THE ART GROUP

DISCOVER YOUR CREATIVE PASSION

J A CRAWSHAW

XYLEM
Publishing

Published by XYLEM Publishing

Copyright © 2023 by J A Crawshaw

All rights reserved.

No part of this book may be reproduced in any form or by any electronic or mechanical means, including information storage and retrieval systems, without written permission from the author, except for the use of brief quotations in a book review.

The moral right of the author has been asserted.

ISBN: 978-1-7394071-3-1 Paperback

ISBN: 978-1-7394071-4-8 Ebook

The author and publisher will have no liability or responsibility to any person or entity regarding any loss, damage or injury incurred, or alleged to have incurred, directly or indirectly, by the information contained in this book. All characters and events within this book are fictitious, and any resemblance to real persons, living or dead is purely coincidental.

Editor: Jill French

Proof Reader: Sarah James

Cover: Xylem Publishing

❦ Created with Vellum

CONTENTS

1.	Dilemma	1
2.	The Bomb Jones	5
3.	Ravish Me	9
4.	Over My Dead Body	13
5.	First Session	17
6.	Session Two	23
7.	Session Three	29
8.	Session Four	35
9.	Dad	41
10.	Session Five	47
11.	Session Six	53
12.	Session Seven	59
13.	Carmen Miranda	63
14.	Session Eight	69
15.	The Secret	79
16.	Early Finish	85
17.	Dad's Words	89
18.	Session Nine	93
19.	Killer Heels	97
20.	I Know What You're Thinking	101
	About the Author	107
	Also by J A Crawshaw	109

THE ART GROUP

DISCOVER YOUR CREATIVE PASSION

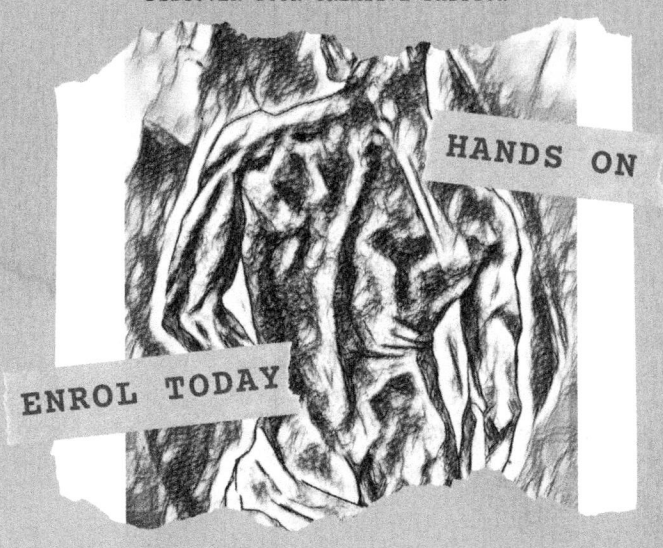

HANDS ON

ENROL TODAY

★ **WANTED** ★

• TUES 7-10PM •

JOIN US AND EXPLORE NEW AND EXCITING POSSIBILITIES

1

DILEMMA

I wasn't expecting it. In fact, I wasn't even looking for it. I'm happily married. Although, I am beginning to realise that just when you think you have all your ducks in a row, life has the audacity to throw you a tidal wave of uncertainty. And in my case, a big dilemma.

It all started when Sarah asked if I'd like to accompany her to a concert. Nothing unusual there, we're great friends and go back a long way. It was her skillful bag-swinging technique that rescued me from the hair-pulling clutches of Marcella Dent, back in junior school, and sealed the deal to forging our long-lasting friendship.

Marcella never intimidated me again which was fortunate as her reputation preceded her. Dent by name, dent by nature, she was a biter as well as a hair puller and her foul mouth and hateful sneer, thankfully, never crossed my path again.

Sarah and I are both forty-three, although she is closer to forty-four and starting to grey a little, she has managed to stay slim, and, at times a little too slim, in my opinion. While I yo-yo diet and calorie count in a futile attempt to regain my youthful physique, she just looks amazing. Some kid on a scooter, the other day, shouted, 'get out of the way you fat lump' and it crushed me to the point I starved myself for three days. Then ended it all, by destroying a whole macadamia cheesecake and a warm bottle of Muscadet, I found lurking at the back of the cupboard.

I hide my curves well and usually only wear black. Paul says he loves me whatever size I am, which is lovely, but I still think he would prefer it if I was a size 12.

That brings me on nicely to family life.

We've been married for seventeen years, and life is busy. Ella is in her final year at school and a high flyer, like Paul. Josh, has two years to go and is academically more like me. We know he's dyslexic and struggles to keep up in class. Ella is a bit of a bookworm and the sort of person who understands everything first time and is eager to move on quickly, while Josh takes his time, and is more arty than any of us. Saying that, I have a talent. You know, for art, but I don't have the time these days to do anything with it.

Paul works hard and we have a great life. In fact, he's just been offered a promotion and we're already talking about maybe getting a place in the Algarve. He loves his golf, so it's the perfect place, and as long as the kids are happy and I have something cold in hand by the pool, I'm not fussy. Although I will never touch Muscadet again, that's for sure. Far too messy.

Anyway, when I say fussy. I mean, somewhere classy of course. Nice places to go for dinner, live music perhaps, and shopping. There's one place we like. It's within walking distance of the clubhouse and even has its own pool.

I work in a bank part-time, it's dull work to be honest, but the girls I work with are good fun. They're the only thing which keeps me there, apart from the money, of course, which pays for most of the kids' stuff and a little extra for me.

Shoes – my Achilles heel. I can't resist, and no one can deny, the right shoes for the right occasion, can make you feel amazing. I'd rather have a new pair of shoes over a handbag any day.

So that's where my dilemma lies. Do I say yes and go to Paris? And if so which shoes? Did I mention Paris? I don't think I did. That's not the concert, but something entirely different, which I will come to shortly.

My dad always says, 'A life without dilemmas is not a life at all. It means you have reached a junction, and have a decision to make, rather than being stayed and stagnant.'

I never really understood as a girl, and to be honest, I still don't, because who likes a dilemma, really? The stress of worrying about making the wrong choice is crippling for me sometimes. I've not told anyone about it. Not even Sarah, and I mean, I tell her everything and she does me. She even confided in me when she spiked her mother-in-law's tea with laxative, which resulted in a week in hospital, with suspected bowel cancer! She's been tempted to do it again on numerous occasions, but I told her, it's too obvious now. I suggested crushing a sleeping tablet in it instead, might be a better way to shut her up. The problem is, her husband isn't very supportive and fails to see that his mother is an interfering old witch. Her words, not mine!

We talk about everything. Well, nearly everything! I don't know why I'm being so cagey about it. It's only for three nights. Not exactly a two-week Mediterranean cruise.

I'm just not sure how Paul will react. I don't want him jumping to conclusions or losing the plot over such a trivial thing, and, Mum's been probing. She's always been perceptive *and* nosey. She said the other day I was looking flush, whatever that means. And that I had a youthful spring in my step she hadn't seen since Harry Glover, the boy next door, gave me those rude letters and a daisy chain. I wore that daisy chain for the rest of the school holidays, despite it going limp and shrivelling up. The thing is, she has a secret. A secret, she doesn't even know I know about.

Anyway. As I said. It all started when Sarah asked if I wanted to go to the concert.

2

THE BOMB JONES

'He's The Bomb Jones.'

'What do you mean?' I said, looking at her as if she were speaking another language.

'The Bomb Jones. Everyone's heard of him. You know, 'Delilah', 'Green, green grass ...', 'Sex bomb' and all that.'

'Do you mean Tom Jones?'

Sarah laughed. 'He's not the real one. He's a tribute. But by all accounts, he sounds just like him and apparently his hips have a mind of their own.'

In disbelief, I tried to compute a rare night out, and one I'd have to sneak past Paul, so I could watch The Bomb Jones gyrate his way into the hearts and minds of the ageing female population of our town.

'A tribute?'

'Yes, but he's good and everyone throws their knickers at him.'

I stopped nodding and my bottom jaw slowly gravitated

toward the floor. 'What! At some old bloke, who's pretending to be the real thing?'

Sarah's face didn't falter. 'So, are you coming or not?'

～

I wanted to hang fire at the back, but Sarah insisted we go to the front. The Bomb came on like he owned the place and with a few grunts and a 'Hello ladies,' an array of undergarments nearly knocked him off his Cuban winkle pickers.

'Here,' Sarah said, clutching something in her hand. 'I brought some for you. Two pairs, just in case you miss first time.'

My heart sank as she handed me two pairs of fuchsia-pink lace knickers.

'I put a pebble in the gusset, because last time, my throw fell short and ended up in the orchestra pit,' she said with all seriousness.

'If that hits him, it'll knock him clean out,' I said looking at the walnut-sized pebble.

She rummaged in her bag and produced the exact same but in red. 'Got these from that holiday we had in Brighton,' she said holding up the second round, sandy-coloured pebble.

'I can't believe you planned ahead, especially for this event.'

'I didn't. These were from a game we played with the kids, to find the most interesting pebble on the beach. I found them in Josh's forgotten-about collection, under his bed. Anyway, wait until he does 'Sex bomb' and then we'll throw.'

I clutched my arsenal tight as he began his opening number and gradually, I felt the surprise and bewilderment in my face turn into a warm smile. He was actually very good and, despite his wig nearly coming off twice, he belted out the numbers in style.

'Sex bomb' was about fifth in his repertoire and with a wink from Sarah, we hurled our projectiles straight at him. He somehow managed to catch Sarah's knickers, and then proceeded to dangle them in front of him as he sang. I was less lucky, and cringed as I watched mine, in slow motion, thump against his knee, causing him to wobble and scowl. The hilarious thing was, it just looked like part of his routine.

What a night! We hadn't had so much fun in years and when Paul picked us up close to midnight, we were still laughing and re-enacting our valiant throws, much to Paul's bemusement.

As we turned the corner into Sarah's road, her mood seemed to change. No more giggles and quips at The Bomb Jones's expense, but a more sombre disposition and a notably pressured brow.

'You alright? Will Lee be home?'

She hesitated. 'He'll be home. I'm fine. Just hope he hasn't been drinking too much.'

I broke the uncomfortable silence which followed. 'Do you want Paul and I to come in with you?'

She shook her head. 'No. I'll be fine. It's just I texted to say we were on our way and I haven't had a reply. He's probably asleep.'

Paul agreed we would wait outside until we received a signal she was okay and, shortly after we dropped her, she waved happily from the bedroom window and gave an encouraging thumbs up.

3

RAVISH ME

Paul and I had a bust up. I confronted him about working late most evenings and leaving me to basically manage the entire house, kids and hold down my own job. He said that money doesn't grow on trees and he was doing his best to provide a good standard of living for us and to start appreciating him more.

I felt bad, because I could see his point, but was still miffed that he failed to see my viewpoint. The real issue for me was that often he didn't get home until after 10 pm and it's starting to become a regular thing. I know what you're thinking, but he's not the kind of guy to have an affair. He's no romantic, that's for sure. I mean, the occasional meal out and flowers on my birthday is as far as it goes, and I still have to drop hints. There aren't any surprises or spontaneous acts of passion, so I doubt anyone else is getting anything either.

Sarah said she thinks he's a bit dull, but what does she

know? She doesn't live with him. The kids adore him and he does spend time with them when he can, and we do have some lovely holidays.

I know he's at the golf club at least once a week and some weekends. That's been a regular since I've known him, and I respect it's his way of switching off.

Anyway, we got a few things off our chests, and I apologised to make peace, saying I appreciated everything he did for our family. I got the kids up to bed early and initiated a bit of 'us' time by putting on my satin nighty and donning a bit of lipstick. I was hoping he might ravish me, like he used to do before we had kids.

I changed back into my comfy pyjamas and glugged back a large G&T not long after, as he said he was shattered.

'Do you still fancy me?' I asked as I pirouetted in my slippers.

He lifted his face out of his laptop. 'Of course I do. You know that.'

I glugged back some more gin. 'I don't ... I think you've gone off me?' I said.

'Don't be daft,' he said looking back at his computer. 'It's, just ... you know how busy life is right now.'

My lead-weighted thoughts took me to the back of his mum's car when we first met, and the giggles we shared as the task of removing my tights within the confines of a Ford Fiesta were entertaining and fruitful. He seemed so manly then, taking control and eventually ripping them with his hands and then bending me over so that my face nudged up against the speaker on the parcel shelf.

I longed for that again. Not particularly in the back of a small hatchback, but at least on the sofa of our sitting room.

THE ART GROUP

It was then, Sarah called and asked if I could get an evening pass the following Tuesday to accompany her to a new art group teaching session she'd seen advertised in the Co-op window. I knew she was wanting to get out of the house even more than usual, but I just couldn't see how I could fit it in.

'Pleeeease,' she said in that puppy-dog voice of hers, and, although I couldn't see them, I felt the draft of her fluttering eyelashes too, which instantly made me feel bad for thinking I couldn't make it.

She continued. 'Look, you know things aren't great between me and Lee. I just need to get out a few nights a week or we're going to strangle each other.'

'Crikey! Is it that bad?'

'You know what he's like. He's adorable until he's had a few drinks. He's out on a Tuesday evening and I'd rather not be sat home alone waiting for the devil to return.'

'Oh Sarah. Why don't you just leave him?'

She cut me off instantly. 'I can't, I don't know why, I just can't.'

'I'm worried for you,' I said with a sigh.

'I can manage him, but I need to be able to get out when I know I need to.'

'Why don't you come and stay with us for a while? Give yourself some thinking time.'

Sarah paused. 'You have enough to deal with and no spare bedroom. Look, thanks, I appreciate the offer, but I'll be fine. Anyway, it will be good for us to open up our creative minds again after all these years. Please say you'll come with me to the art group.'

'First, passing art at school doesn't constitute a creative

mind, and second, I need to run this by Paul as I don't think he's going to be too happy.'

'So, is that a yes then?'

4

OVER MY DEAD BODY

Tuesday evenings weren't ideal. I didn't finish until 5.30pm, but the kids were letting themselves in now, so I didn't have to stress about that.

I asked Paul to be back before half six so that I could make the 7pm start.

Sarah's a fifteen-minute drive away and she said she'd meet me there. At first, I felt like I was going out of duty, so that she could get her head straight about Lee. They got married two years before us and have no kids, but I feel like it's probably the beginning of the end for them.

Anyway, we always have a laugh, especially when we're out and, to be frank, I was looking for something to challenge my brain. So I thought, why not? I hardly ever go out in the week and if I'm completely honest, felt like it would do me good not to be a wife and mother, one evening a week.

I became quite excited about doing some art again. I even set up a little home studio. Well, a lovely wooden easel, some textured paper, a set of brushes and paints I had stashed in the wardrobe for the last six or seven years.

We only ever use the dining room at Christmas and the kids used to have birthday parties in there, but those days seem over now. So I folded the table down to its smallest, put in two of the six chairs from the garage and erected the easel, which had been acting as a clothes horse since we moved to the house. It's hardly a Parisian penthouse overlooking the Seine, but a view of the garden was just fine and I always have something interesting and colourful growing in the greenhouse. Tomatoes, sunflowers or geraniums.

I set it all up one afternoon and then just stared at the paper for about ten minutes. Don't know whether I gave myself too much pressure or I'd just lost my artistic ability. Anyway, after gazing out of the window for another five minutes, making a coffee and putting a load of washing on, I came back to it and just had a go at what was in front of me.

The smell of the paints took me straight back to school and I was both nervous and excited about applying the brush and making a start.

A blackbird fluttered around the garden and then into the apple tree. The blossom had taken on a pinky, white hue in the spring sun, which drew my eye.

There was something liberating about indulging in a couple of hours of just me time. It felt like only ten minutes, but it was freedom.

The kids were interested for a minute because the dining room had changed function. Ella was concerned we wouldn't be having Christmas again and Josh was upset as apparently he'd discussed with Paul about putting a snooker table in there. *Over my dead body!*

Anyway, I made Sunday roast and we enjoyed a glass of Malbec, before I presented my painting.

I think I was most disappointed about the way Paul laughed. Not so much, the laughing itself. It was a very amateur attempt and as I said, I hadn't done any art since leaving school. But he sounded condescending, as if I shouldn't be wasting my time with such triviality. Well, he said pretty much that. 'Didn't I have better things to be doing, like tidying the garage?' To be fair, I had been promising to do that for months and he was right. There were more important things to be doing and wasting time on painting was not going to get the laundry clean and dry.

My mixed emotions and the three of them ganging up on me made me upset, but I tried not to show it. The evening ended in a bit of a shouting match, with the kids seizing the opportunity to wade in with their demands on the room and Paul seemingly backing them. Eventually, I conceded and packed up my easel and paints and swapped them again with the chairs from the garage. It was a good thing really. Peace in the house and a reminder to sort the garage sooner than later.

5

FIRST SESSION

I was clock watching right up until the bank doors locked at five thirty and then hotfooted it home for a shower and spruce up. I wasn't sure what to wear, but Sarah said she was taking the casual approach with jeans and a T-shirt, so I agreed that was probably best for an arty session involving paints and the like. My Converse seemed the natural accompaniment and together with my blue scarf which Ella bought me for Christmas and my black duvet coat, I was out of the door and on my way into the chilly evening.

I left the kids watching TV and Paul just about made it in the door for my timely getaway. He showed up with a Chinese takeaway and they promised to save me some fried rice and a few sweet and sour balls for my return.

Sarah met me in the car park.

'So he let you out, then?' she said, hugging me.

'I could say the same to you. How's it going?'

She released her grip. 'Let's not talk about that now.

Let's go and do some art.' I could see she was trying her best to forget about home and let her hair down.

～

I had no idea the Arts Centre had so much going on. It was a busy venue and from the notice board by the entrance, there were dance, music, drama and our beginner's art class all happening on the same evening. Sarah clocked there was a bar and tweaked my arm to tip me off. 'Let's hope we get a break halfway through,' she said, raising her tattooed brow.

My set back at home left me a little uneasy about becoming involved in the group. I was eager to get some paints out and start being creative, yet concerned I was neglecting my family. It also felt naughty being out on a school night.

The room was set out like a classroom. A desk in the far centre, a whiteboard, harsh fluorescent lighting, and wooden tables and chairs. I was expecting easels and a studio with paint all over the floor, but Sarah and I settled into our chosen seats. I wanted to sit by the window, but Sarah chose differently because of a man on his own, with wild blond hair and eyes which tracked our every move as soon as we stepped in. I hadn't seen him, but Sarah was on the ball.

My quick arithmetic suggested there were probably fifteen or sixteen others, plus a very efficient-looking, schoolmarm-type lady sorting papers at the main desk in front of us. She kept peering over her glasses and then returned to organising whatever needed organising.

Sarah and I chatted nervously. I can't remember what

THE ART GROUP

exactly, just stuff to make us feel like we weren't on our own or prey for the wild-haired and slightly intimidating man.

Eventually, Ruth introduced herself and started handing out the paperwork and calling out the names on the register, which simultaneously confirmed you'd paid the correct fee and were accepted into the class. It felt like we were back in Mrs Henderson's art class from all those years back. She was an old battle-axe and used to peer over her specs, usually in disgust or contempt, and always when I was passing a note or chewing some gum.

I was chewing involuntarily at the thought and had a very slight impulse to be naughty. If only I had my old ruler and some tissue balls! Anyway, Sarah gave me a look which told me she was thinking exactly the same and we giggled between ourselves.

I listened to all the names and put them to the corresponding faces.

Lucy and Emily. They were young girls, early twenties probably, and looked like younger versions of Sarah and me.

Aisha and Lila sat together and didn't speak a word. Sweet girls was my instant judgement, due to their matching pigtails and freckled faces.

Mel and Trudy looked like art students. Trudy's mass of blonde hair had streaks of blue and purple and was being tamed at the back with an equally colourful silk scarf, and Mell wore magenta dungarees and carried off a skinhead haircut and numerous piercings.

Trevor was the guy we spotted straight away sat on his own. Every time I looked at him, he was staring back. Although his replies, in contrast, seemed posh and polite, instinctively, we knew he was one to avoid.

Evelyn sat on her own. Pru Leith was the first thing that entered my head and I mouthed it to Sarah. Older and sophisticated in thick black tights, a respectful, just below the knee skirt and red cashmere jumper gave a confident and assured look.

Pam and Eric were, I assumed, husband and wife. I could have been wrong, but they seemed comfortable together and he pulled out the chair for Pam. And they sat close and chatted calmly.

Sandra and Patty both wore an array of jewellery, with bangles running up both arms, rings on every finger and jet-black hair perched high on their heads tied in colourful ribbons. Patty seemed to find everything amusing and her deep, fun-loving, soulful laugh soon started to lighten the mood of the room, much to Ruth's disapproval.

Dan was a quiet lad. Art student if I had to make a guess. Thin with pale skin, but a funny looking black streak in his alba-white hair.

Last but not least was Dave. He sat on his own and appeared friendly. Younger than me by maybe six or seven years? It was hard to tell. He had a youthful face, but the demeanour and confidence of someone older. He introduced himself when we first arrived, while chatting with Pam and Eric, as well as joining in with Patty's infectious deep cackles.

Sarah turned to me and smiled. 'Interesting bunch,' she said under her breath.

I acknowledged with a smile.

Ruth eventually finished the administration and proceeded to set out the structure of the sessions, which to Sarah's delight did include a fifteen-minute break while the bar was open and that all the art materials were included as part of the fee.

What I couldn't work out, was that Ruth didn't look arty at all. I couldn't imagine her inspiring anyone to run amok with acrylics or Lino prints! Had we come to the right course? I thought as she looked stern, rebuffing any of Patty's joviality.

It was only then, that Ruth announced that Mr Devonish, the artist who would be teaching us, wasn't able to attend that evening, due to a family commitment and that he would be taking over the reins the following week. She also said that he had requested we all bring something which meant something to us, to the next session. It could be anything which was important to us is some way.

6

SESSION TWO

Paul wasn't impressed that I'd gone to an art class and come away having done nothing. He said, 'I don't know why you're wasting your time with a bunch of hippies.'

I said, 'I had little chance to meet them all, but they seemed like lovely people, and why was he being so judgemental?'

I think he was upset that he had to finish work at what I thought was a reasonable hour for a change, and that there was no dinner on the table. They didn't even leave me any pork balls, so I had a bowl of Rice Krispies instead and pondered silently what item I might take with me the following week.

Anyway, I wasn't working the following day, so I made Paul get the kids off to school and I just laid in bed, thinking. There wasn't a sound. No lawnmowers, no tree surgeons with leaf blowers, not even a car. Just silence. Blissful silence. I realised perfectly what they mean by 'silence can be deafening'. I always thought that was just a clever line from a song and never really gave it much thought. But silence has a ring to it and different tones and depth and resonance. Now, before you think I'm going insane, try it. It's freaky, but liberating. Just taking the time out of life to hear nothing, and furthermore to enjoy it, started me thinking about, just that, life. You know, perspectives and feelings, that kind of thing. I don't normally have time to dwell, but I was trying to be mindful. I'd read somewhere that was the *done thing* these days.

The thing is. I knew my mum's secret and I'd been holding back for some time about whether to say something. It all came to a head when she came around for breakfast. Not her usual visiting time, but she was on her way back from the hospital, as dad was not very well.

I made pancakes and she told me he'd been having tests after finding blood in his urine. It had been going on a while but intermittent, and he'd chosen to ignore it. He only told her a few weeks ago.

It's at times like this, you realise no one's really telling the truth! Look at Sarah, she's pretty much living a lie. Lee isn't a nice guy, but she can't afford to move out and if I'm honest with myself, I suspect Paul isn't always working late. But I have the kids to think about, and we don't want to be destitute.

So mum goes on to tell me about her health scare. She'd been feeling dizzy and her vision keeps blurring. The doctor has suggested it's probably related to high blood pressure, and he's prescribed a calcium channel blocker; I think she said.

She's been getting stressed at little things so I've been

THE ART GROUP

holding off talking to her about my dilemma. The problem is ... something needs to be said, and I can't hold it in much longer.

Tuesday came, and I was excited about the art group. I decided to take two things. I couldn't decide between them, so I thought I'd push my luck. The first thing was a beaker both the kids had drunk from when they were little. Water and then juice and you could see the marks made by their tiny teeth on the spout. It held fond memories of day trips and playing in the park, so I kept it.

The second thing was a framed photograph of my father. The faded colour picture was of him wearing a suit and smoking a cigarette, leaning against a huge car. It was taken some forty or so years previous. He looked young and had a full head of dark brown hair, just like me. I ran my hand through my hair and then traced my cheekbone with my finger. He had very pronounced cheekbones and a dimple in his chin. I didn't have the dimple, but I was glad about that.

Sarah met me in the car park. She was flustered and said she nearly didn't make it. I noticed she had gone over the top with her foundation and blusher, again.

We entered the room to find most of the others already at their seats and no sooner had we taken to ours, Sarah gave the raised eyebrow alert. 'Incoming, 3 o'clock,' she said, with all the skills of a ventriloquist.

Trevor was making a beeline and there was no escape.

'Hello ladies,' he said. 'I didn't get a chance to introduce myself last week. I'm Trevor, but most people call me Trev.' He leaned awkwardly on our table.

Sarah's eyes met with mine, and we felt instinctively

each other's entire organs cringing. No one had ever called him Trev! Not with grey slacks and Hush Puppy shoes.

He held out his hand. Sarah shook it first, then me. It was clammy and smooth and his smile was too.

'I normally work in oils, but I'm here to broaden my horizons. What about you?'

Sarah didn't hesitate with her reply. 'We're out on licence. It was this or some other kind of rehab. She bludgeoned her ex-husband to death with a lump hammer, and I prefer throwing electrical items into baths.'

I looked at her in complete disbelief. Where the hell did that come from?

'You're still wearing your wedding ring though,' he said, looking down at my hand.

It was then, the door flung open and in strode, who we could only assume was Mr Devonish. The urgent gust of air which followed him was infused with musky spiced bergamot, sage, and wood smoke, which made me instantly relax and take note.

We watched him as his black jacket appeared cape-like as he headed to the front. The only other thing visible was his thick salt and pepper hair from the back. Jet black, with natural silver streaks.

I looked at Sarah and she looked at me. 'I wonder what his family commitments were?' she muttered under her breath, subconsciously brushing her lips with her finger and removing her ring.

We watched him casually throw armfuls of paper onto his desk and then remove his jacket to reveal a light blue cotton shirt with the top three buttons undone. He cast his eyes around the room as he roughly folded his sleeves to reveal his tanned and hairy forearms. We looked at each other again, but this time without words.

We hadn't even noticed slimy Trev disappearing back to his seat, as Mr Devonish brandished a marker pen and wrote on the whiteboard, in bold letters, 'ART'.

Then he spoke. 'Art! What is art?' His tones were deep and sure, like liquid velvet wrapped around solid mahogany. No time for introductions, obviously! Just straight into it, like an artistic gun-slinger who'd just rode into town.

I so wanted to answer, but kept quiet and so did everyone else, except Sarah.

'It's painting and sculpture, and expressing yourself,' she said toying with her hair.

He looked at her and pointed his pen. 'Mmmm. Interesting. It's Sarah, isn't it?' he said smiling back at her. 'Anyone else?'

Trev tried his luck. 'It's our own representation of what we see.'

'Mmmmmm,' he said tapping the pen on his chin. 'Anyone else?'

Evelyn raised her hand. 'I think it's a way of showing what's important to us, like our feelings. Our hopes and fears.'

He put both his hands on his desk and leaned forward, while maintaining eye contact with her. 'Now we're getting somewhere. Evelyn.'

His wood-smoky-brown eyes sparkled as he looked at each one of us. *How did he know our names?*

'Art is the expression of the soul in its purest form. It is a bridge between the tangible and the intangible, capturing emotion and thought in a single moment. Art is a way to share our stories, emotions and ideas, and an exploration into the depths of the human experience, allowing us to see our own lives and the world around us. It is not limited by time or space, but instead transcends them, allowing us to explore our innermost thoughts and feelings in a unique and powerful way.'

'Oh shit!' Sarah said, fanning her flushed face with her hand.

7

SESSION THREE

Of course, our drawings of our special items were appalling. Sarah had forgotten to bring anything, so she ended up with my children's beaker and I attempted to draw my father, who appeared to lean against a Sherman tank rather than an old Cortina.

I waited for Sarah in the car park, and with minutes to spare before the start of the session; she rolled up in what were probably the tightest figure-hugging black leather trousers I have ever seen. Even Olivia Newton-John would have been shocked at the way they left very little to the imagination. To compliment, a low-cut blouse which was all but see-through and a crimson lace bra pushing everything up like an erupting volcano.

'Sorry I'm late. I underestimated curling my hair. Do you like it?'

I remember doing that half nod, half shake of my head thing and assuming an unconvincing smile.

'I wonder what he'll be wearing tonight?'

'Who?' I asked.

'Mr Art himself. The devilish, Devonish.'

'So that's what this is all about?'

'I can't tell you how inspiring he is. I haven't stopped thinking about him all week.'

'Well, let's hope we're not brass rubbing tonight,' I said, watching her boobs enter the room before both of us.

Everyone's eyes followed Sarah's various lumps and bumps to her seat and Mr Devonish gave a courteous smile, before holding up Evelyn's painting, from the previous session, of a solitary beach hut, windswept and tatty in places from the weather, it stood alone on the edge of the sand. 'Can you talk us through your choice of painting, Evelyn?' he said warmly.

My eyes were drawn to Evelyn's seamed stockings, heels and hair, up in a mischievous, slightly unravelling bun. A complete contrast to her humble and slightly demure presence the previous week. I looked around at everyone else and, with no exception, they all had either upped their colour profile to the next shade of 'look at me' or dug out their most revealing, or expressive outfits.

I instantly felt fat and frumpy. I was in my baggy, slightly sun-bleached white T-shirt and blue jeans from before, in the naïve assumption, we were there to do art and get messy!

In my feeble attempt to hide as much of my body under the table as possible, I knocked over my bag and the contents spilled out on the floor by Dave's feet.

By the time I'd managed to prize myself out of my chair,

THE ART GROUP

Dave had gallantly rescued the bag and contents, and placed them on the table. He smiled, and I noticed his lovely teeth. 'Thanks,' I said

'It's my pleasure,' he replied, as I noticed his glinting green eyes and a warm kindness in his voice.

It was then, the hell, which was worse than any humiliation I had ever experienced, hit me with the force of a double-decker bus, as Dave reached to the floor one more time and then held up the skimpy fuchsia knickers, the spare, pair, I still had in my bag from The Bomb Jones gig.

My instant reaction was to look as bemused as he did and pretend everything was cool, when inside, I was wrenching my intestines. Mr Devonish appeared to the side of me and Sarah grabbed the offending item, as he came close to scrutinise the chaos of the contents of my bag. The sight of Sarah clutching sexy knickers, with almost a fully exposed bosom, and Dave grinning like a Cheshire cat, made the whole class stare and me blush more.

Mr Devonish then showed his true persona. With dignity, poise and with a confident, unflustered tone, he broadcast to the entire group. 'Colour is the life! Light is the depth and texture is the meaning.' His eyes never faltering from Sarah's face. 'Art is passion and passion is life.'

Sarah nearly orgasmed on the spot. You could see a red flush rising across her shoulders and neck, making her bosom look ripe and almost edible.

I scuttled everything back into my bag and felt the presence of Mr Devonish leave my side and replaced with a sincere apology from Dave and a sympathetic smile. I just wanted the world to swallow me up.

My forlorn silence was broken when Patty burst into hysterical laughter when Mr Devonish held up her painting of two coconuts, which she said reminded her of being a girl back in Jamaica. No one dared look at Sarah, especially me, but Patty's infectious laugh seemed to bring everyone together. The presentation of everyone's artwork and their explanations of why they were important to them, became enjoyable insights as Mr Devonish discussed individual styles and mediums used. Sadly, the pain for me was not over when he held up my drawing of my father.

'Why is this important to you?' he said with an inquisitive air.

I gulped and my arms shook. I couldn't get any words out and beads of sweat gathered on my forehead. 'Is it someone you know?'

It felt like my throat was in my mouth. I couldn't speak. Mr Devonish's face appeared compassionate and wise. 'If it's too personal to share, then that's absolutely fine. I wanted to comment on how you have captured the timing of this scene with your pencil. Although it's black and white, the light on the gentleman's face, and the reflections on the car bodywork are quite splendid. But what I like the most is the angst on his face. You can see he is posing for a photo and trying to look calm, yet we see his brow and shoulders pressured by torment. Am I right?'

I took a very deep breath. 'The man is my father. And, yes. He had a troubled life. I only wish ...' I felt Sarah's eyes digging into me as I let down my protective guard and broke into tears.

Mr Devonish was once again by my side and held a box

of tissues. He took one and handed it to me. 'It's a very beautiful drawing. I could feel the sentiment within the pencil strokes,' he said, handing me another tissue and then concluding the session.

8

SESSION FOUR

Mum had popped round again, but later in the day. She'd been to the hospital again and was angry this time that I hadn't been. I blamed it on work and the kids. Ballet and rugby sessions combined demanded a lot from the taxi of mum.

It was no excuse though, and she knew it. I was about to tell her the truth, when Paul came breezing in with a brand-new set of golf clubs.

He already had three sets, so I challenged him.

'If we are getting that villa in Portugal, I need to not only be up to par with the lads, but all the other high flyers out there too. By the way, speaking of the lads. We're heading out there on a bit of a reccy mission, in a few weeks. Hope that's okay.'

Well, what could I say? It didn't look like it was up for discussion. Anyway, a reccy mission with or without me sounded promising and to be honest, I was beginning to enjoy my evening out with Sarah and the art group and didn't really want to miss a session.

'When is it?'

'Oh I don't know. In a few weeks. We have to get a date when everyone can make it.'

∼

I waited for Sarah. She was late, and the class was about to start. Abandoning the car park, I decided to go in without her. I entered to find everyone gathered around Patty, who was telling a story about when she was invited to meet the Queen at her garden party. An award for community projects, from what I could gather from my late entry. Anyway, in the wait for Mr Devonish everyone, including Trevor, joined in with Patty's infectious laughter over shoe heel malfunctions and awkward canapé and drink mishaps when trying to maintain a level of dignity.

Mr Devonish entered like a whirlwind. His jacket, differently coloured each week, and always playing catchup with him, as he flew along in haste.

A last-minute text from Sarah reassured me she wasn't dead in a ditch somewhere, but nevertheless, gave her apologies that she would not make it. I didn't have time to reply, as Mr Devonish instructed us to erect an easel each, install a piece of paper and collect a pack of charcoal sticks from his desk.

I had a bit of an issue with my easel. For some reason, I couldn't lock it in position and it kept trying to close up on itself. Dave gallantly lent a hand and, with a bit of brute force, managed to slide in the locking pin and secure

THE ART GROUP

it in place. 'It's a nightmare when you have a problem with your erection!' he said, pretending to dust off his hands.

I looked at him and then we both laughed. His smile set me off. He had a cheekiness about him, which was endearing.

Mr Devonish instructed us to get into pairs. Well, I was still having my moment with Dave, and somehow, by default, we agreed to joining forces. Where was bloody Sarah when I needed her the most?

'Okay everyone. *Charcoal.*' Mr Devonish said dramatically.

'Has anyone worked with charcoal before?' he asked as he finished erecting his own easel and then proceeded to walk around the room, making sure everyone had all the relevant equipment.

Mel, Trudy and Evelyn raised their hands. I had messed around with charcoal at school, but chose not to create any expectation and kept quiet. Dave had already been into his pack of charcoals and unbeknown to him, somehow managed to put a black smudge on his top lip and, with his dark side-parted hair, looked just like a comical version of everyone's not so favourite Fascist dictator. I couldn't stop laughing, which drew the attention of the others and once Patty started laughing, well, that was it. The only one not laughing was Dave until I showed him the photo I took on my phone.

'Okay. Joking apart. I want you in your pairs to sketch portraits of each other.' Everyone groaned, apart from Evelyn, who had no choice other than to team up with Trevor. Anyway, before anyone else picked up their charcoals, Evelyn was cracking on with a confident look and a carefree hand.

I was happy that I hadn't been saddled with Trevor, but soon came to realise I wasn't going to be able to concentrate. Dave, in his attempts to clean off the charcoal from his top lip, with a tissue from my emergency supply, had managed to distribute it further around his face and was quickly taking on the appearance of a coal miner. I couldn't stop laughing. I stared at the floor in an attempt to contain myself, and the moment I looked at him, he set me off again.

It worsened, when I tried to help him and then it went all over my face! We laughed so much, my sides ached, and my jaw started to cramp.

If you think it couldn't get any worse, I nearly peed myself when I peered around his easel and saw what was supposed to be me, looking like a pin head gerbil with huge ears on a massive body. I had to go to the ladies and calm myself down by splashing cold water on my face and cooling off under the hand dryer.

Oh Lord, Dave was a funny man. I hadn't laughed that much in years. In fact, I couldn't remember the last time.

On returning, I decided to get a grip of myself and try and make the best effort I could. The charcoals felt easy in my hand. I liked the way I could use them to shade and then further distribute the pigment with my finger. Mr Devonish had been coaching everyone individually, and eventually he arrived at my easel.

'Lovely,' he said, looking at my drawing with a slightly tilted head. 'I like your interpretation of light and shade once again.'

THE ART GROUP

I looked at Dave and shrugged.

Then, Mr Devonish came in close to my shoulder. I could smell his woody, smoky aftershave, and it made me go slightly heady. He then took my hand and started gently creating strokes on the paper. My hand holding the charcoal and his hand holding mine. I don't know what happened, but it made me go weak at the knees and my heart rate seemed to triple. *Jeez!* The energy from that man was incredible. I could feel myself getting hotter and hotter, but I was locked in. Unable to move, and tingling from head to toe. He concentrated on one spot, working the charcoal deep into the paper and then, while interlocking his fingers into mine, we rubbed together. Rubbing and stroking together rhythmically. What the hell was happening? I felt uncomfortable, yet did not want it to stop. He looked at me. 'See how we created the illusion of depth and intrigue with just a few simple strokes?'

I just gasped. His voice was like liquid honey and his eyes like cinnamon-infused tobacco leaves, mixed with sweet chestnut and hazel.

Wow! I didn't know what had hit me, but I knew I wanted more.

9

DAD

I didn't know what was wrong with me. I just couldn't concentrate, and not only that, I was niggly and tearful.

I just felt a bit taken for granted. The kids had their homework in the evenings, but with a little nagging, they generally did something to help around the house. Josh more than Ella to be honest. Although she's bright, she could be a complete lazybones given the chance. She's diligent about her homework, but her room was a disgrace. Clothes, makeup, bowls with rotting food stuffed under the bed and just a lack of pride. Josh and I tended to chat in the kitchen after dinner. He'd help me with the bins or unloading shopping. Don't get me wrong, his room was not perfect, but at least he'd have a binge tidy-up now and again.

Anyway, it wasn't the kids who were the problem that night. Paul rolled in gone 10pm. I'd had dinner with the kids and I couldn't get hold of him, because I really wanted him to fetch some milk and cheese for the jacket potatoes and some flowers so I could take them to the hospital in the morning, because I wouldn't have time to do everything.

He wasn't answering his phone although I could see he was on and off WhatsApp like a yo-yo. Anyway, like I said, he rolled in, left his shoes and coat on the kitchen floor and collapsed on the sofa complaining of a headache, and could he have his dinner where he was?

It takes a lot to get me angry, but what broke my back was that he'd 'forgotten' to get the things I asked him to bring home. How could I go to the hospital without flowers? I'd have to do a special journey to the express shop, which was in totally the wrong direction. And their flowers were poor, and the parking a nightmare.

I asked him where he'd been.

Apparently, they had the big boss over from America and the whole team had to go out for drinks. No choice, he said. And that it was a dull evening and he was starving.

He wasn't drunk, but he'd had a drink or two. I could smell it on him. Why wasn't he answering his phone, though? Not to mention risking a drink driving ban, which could mean he'd lose his job and put all our lives at risk.

Something wasn't adding up, but he kept saying that I was overreacting and that I was hormonal and needed to chill. When I challenged him again and he told me I was going mad, that made me do what I did. I feel bad about it today, but impulsively, and having only a small corner of cheese left for his potato and cheesy beans, I got a little carried away with the grating and 'accidentally' grated some of the plastic in there too. I melted it joyfully into the mix.

The thing is, there's no arguing with him. It's his way or no

THE ART GROUP

way. One of the things I used to like about him was his confidence and ambition, but now he seemed arrogant and self-centred, and to be honest, I was not liking him very much, so our intimate time had just dropped off a cliff and I missed that.

I told Sarah and in a way I'm grateful I'm not in her position. At least I'm not scared of him. I told her to go to the police, but she says Lee can be very loving and that he's right about her not being able to cope without him. To be honest, I don't really want to know the detail, because it scares me that he'll take it too far. I'm there for her, but I can't go wading in. She'd kill me. She has to make her own decisions.

As I said, I'm not in that position, thankfully, but I still felt hurt. While he was tucking into his 'melted medley', I shifted his shoes from the kitchen and hung his coat up. I didn't mean to go snooping, but as I slipped my hand into the pocket, and found a receipt. It was in her name. Lucy. She must have an account there. The wine bar on Cheapside Road. It's one of the favourite haunts of many of the offices in that area. What was strange, though, was it was for six drinks. Four Proseccos and two Baileys!

There must be at least twenty-five of them in that office, and probably a dozen more I don't know about, so six drinks seemed on the light side. And if it were a corporate event, why in her name? I know who she is. She's relatively new there, three or four months, that's all. Single, no kids, go-getter type with heels as high as her ego and morals as low as her knickers – probably? I didn't like her. Met her at the Christmas bash and she looked down her boney vegan nose at me.

I didn't tell him I'd seen it, just slipped it back in the pocket and left it there.

The following morning, I felt like I could have done with a couple of Proseccos. I grabbed some cheap flowers from the garage instead of backtracking to the shop and headed to the hospital. Mum said she'd meet me there. I felt a bit guilty not going sooner, but I just didn't feel compelled to go. Mum said that Dad was not doing so well and that he was disappointed I hadn't been, or Paul and the kids for that matter.

The thing was, I knew the truth, and I'd known for some time. It's one of those things which had been eating away at me, but I hadn't found the right time to tell her. I guess it was just another one of life's hurdles which are sent to test us. I've laid awake at night. When Paul sleeps in the spare room, because of his snoring, I lay there for hours, mulling it all through and darting from one decision to another and then back again. I had to decide whether it was worth telling the truth or keeping my mouth shut for everyone's sake. The critical thing was ... I knew that nobody knew that I knew mum's secret. It's complicated, obviously, but I made up my mind, and was going to come clean.

I met mum at the entrance, and she took me to see Dad. The flowers were wrapped in cheap plastic and I hadn't even written a card. Once again, I felt on my own. I know mum was there, but I was holding back on telling her. Having Paul by my side would have made me feel better about being there. I approached the bed with thoughts of the holidays we had been on, and how he had taught me to ride a bike. His knowledge of plants and trees was ingrained in my mind, as he always wanted to pass that on, and Mum

THE ART GROUP

was never interested. He was a kind man, with a generous spirit, and I didn't want him potentially going to his grave thinking that, despite his loving heart and devotion to our family, I secretly resented him.

Mum put the flowers in a vase and I held Dad's hand tightly. 'Paul and the kids send their love,' I said. 'I'll bring them on Saturday, if you're up for it?'

His eyes looked weary and he couldn't speak. I could see he probably didn't have long and gave him a sip of water to moisten his lips.

'Thank you for everything you have done for me,' I said, feeling choked. 'You've been the best dad anyone could have wished for.'

10

SESSION FIVE

I spent the whole day feeling rotten about Paul's melted medley. What if the plastic was toxic, and it poisoned him? I texted him relentlessly to the point, he called me, and asked me to stop pestering him, as he was in meetings. I was comforted by his spirit, knowing he was fine, and he reassured me he would be home in time for me to go to the art group.

I was surprised to see Sarah in the car park waiting for me. Gone were the leather pants only to be replaced with a figure-hugging black dress which barely covered her bottom or shoulders.

'Are you going on somewhere after?' I asked.

She looked at me with a smile which said 'help me.'

I raised an eyebrow.

'You never know,' she said. 'Maybe, just maybe, Devilish Devonish will save me from my peril and make me feel wanted again?'

'You don't have to do this, you know. Do you think you're making yourself look ... cheap?'

She shrugged. 'I don't care. I'm beyond feeling good about myself.'

I flung my arms around her and we hugged tight. 'We don't have to go in there tonight.'

She paused. 'I know. But I want to. Do you think I look cheap?'

I maintained my tight grip. 'Of course not. You look amazing. Wish I could slip into something like that. Anyway, I've made the decision, you're moving in with us.'

She pushed herself away. 'I can't do that. What about you, Paul and the kids?'

'You need to get your head straight. We can move things around and Paul can even sleep on the sofa. I'm worried about you.'

Hand in hand, we walked into the building. 'Don't worry about me. I'll be fine. I appreciate the offer and I'm not saying no, but Lee's away for a week and it'll give me some time to think about what's going on.'

With a sigh, I nodded and squeezed her hand tight.

By the time we entered the class, Mr Devonish was already instructing everyone to erect their easels for a watercolour evening. We both got to work and exchanged that special look only best friends can give, knowing this was going to be our evening and whatever crap was happening in our lives; we were going to forget everything and let our creativity go wild.

Individually, we had to paint whatever came into our minds. Mr Devonish continued to talk about freedom of expression and how it was best to let your creative brain

THE ART GROUP

take its own course, and that prescription was the killer of all creativity.

Sarah seemed to be using a lot of black. And as I mixed yellows and orange, I thought about the Algarve and days of warm sun and the kids having fun in the pool.

Dave wasn't there, and I secretly craved his humour as I thought it may have lightened the mood for Sarah. Instead I kept looking over at Devonish. I wanted him to help me again with my light and shadow, and as I watched him, I became fascinated by how he bit his bottom lip in one corner when he was concentrating. He was engrossed with Pam and Eric, helping them mix colours and experiment with different amounts of paint and water.

Lucy and Emily caught my eye as they seemed to have more paint on each other than their paintings. They reminded me of Sarah and myself when we were younger. Naïve but cheeky. Our whole lives ahead of us and not a care. I smiled.

Then the manly scent of Devonish was right behind me. I could feel my heart thumping. I was apprehensive he might touch me again, and what might that do to me?

'Burnt sienna is such a sensual colour isn't it?' he said. His words just like the colour itself. I was hot again and although I knew it was wrong, I liked it and it excited me. For a moment, I imagined him putting his strong arms around me as he took control and the mood switched from the family poolside of the Algarve to the intimate terracotta tiles of Tuscany, and the two of us sharing the passionate and very adult view, as the sun disappeared behind our sparkling glasses of playful Prosecco. We savoured the burnt sienna sun on our naked skin.

His firm hand on my shoulder brought me back into class, and as he brushed past me, I could not only smell his evocative scent, I could smell man. Pheromones. There was something quite thrilling about that man. Maybe his air of mystery and intrigue, or maybe he was all man. I couldn't pin it on one thing. Anyway, as he moved towards Sarah, he commented on how he liked her use of the flat head brush, while taking a glance back at me. His eyes looked with intent, I looked away and mixed some more paint vigorously on my palette.

I don't know why I let him do that to me. I was a married woman and although I was flattered; I told myself I was imagining something far beyond a cursory look and a hand on my shoulder to steady himself. I concentrated on my painting and didn't give him a second thought as I let my hand freely move across the paper in an abstract, yet purposeful, way.

During the break, Sarah and I treated ourselves to a G & T. I felt I needed it, and Sarah didn't need much encouragement.

'I think he fancies me,' Sarah said, slightly under her breath. 'Did you see how he was helping me with my composition? And did you get a whiff of his aftershave?'

I smiled and nodded. 'There's no wedding ring, so I guess free to fancy anyone he wants,' I replied.

She then took a miniature bottle out of her bag and gave us both a top up of gin. 'I always keep a spare,' she said. 'Anyway, you sound a bit jealous.'

'I can assure you, I'm not jealous,' I said sternly. 'There're probably another ten classes just like this, where

THE ART GROUP

he schmoozes with many other unsuspecting and *married*, ladies.'

Sarah nodded, then glugged her drink. 'Have you seen his hands, though? They're big and they're not smooth, like Lee's. He's obviously a hands-on, practical man.'

It was my turn to glug my drink. 'Of course he is. He's a bloody artist. Anyway, why are we talking about him? There are a thousand other things to talk about.'

Sarah gave me that look, that knowing look. 'And I bet he's attentive,' she said before downing the rest of her drink in one.

On returning home, I was eager to show my painting to my biggest fans. I was really delighted by how I'd managed to capture the feel of summer and the shimmer of the sea with a combination of white and azure blue. That was Mr Devonish's idea, which I took on board and, to be honest, it transformed the whole piece.

'Do you like my painting?' I asked as I entered the living room. Josh momentarily lifted his head from his iPad and gave me a thumbs up. Ella had her headphones on and didn't even look up, and Paul scrunched up his face.

'Don't you like it? I thought, with a frame, it might look good in the dining room?'

His face remained scrunched. 'What is it?'

'It's the Algarve. Maybe it could go in pride of place in our new villa?'

Paul took it and turned it upside down, squinting. 'Looks more like the contents of our recycling bin.'

I headed upstairs for a soak in the bath, loaded it with relaxing bubble bath, and lit a candle.

11

SESSION SIX

Mum rang to say Dad was off his monitor and that she hoped he would be home by the end of the week. It was a surprise, and I told her I was glad and suggested I cook a Sunday dinner if he was up to it.

Hearing the news made me determined to face the situation and tell her what I'd been holding in for far too long. I told her I had something to get off my chest and a coffee at the garden centre on my day off would be the perfect time. She suggested coming along to the art group, as she wanted to get some inspiration for a new kitchen she was planning. I nearly choked and in no uncertain terms, told her it wasn't a design class and anyway, she wasn't enrolled and there weren't enough seats. *Jeez*. Imagine my mother in the mix!

I waited impatiently for Sarah, but she never showed. I contemplated ditching the art group and going around to her house to see if she was okay. But then at the last minute, a text saying she was fine, but she had to work late.

I sent a raised eyebrow emoji, and she instantly replied with a red heart and two lines of kisses.

I knew she was trying to placate me. I wasn't happy that she might be in danger and tried to call. Her instant 'I'm in a meeting' response, doing little to put my mind at rest.

Suddenly, Devonish appeared and thrust a large bag into my arms. 'Great timing,' he said, smiling. I could just see his face over the top of another two similar bulging bags. 'I thought we'd play around with textures this week. Evoke a bit of passion into our work.'

We had a 'moment'. One of those few times in your life, where someone looks deep into your eyes and you can feel it in every organ of your body. He had this thing about him which was mesmerising and I couldn't help but be drawn in.

'What's in the bags?' I asked.

'Leather, lace, silk, oh, and some feathers.'

'You must have raided Mrs Devonish's wardrobe?' I said, double-checking his ring finger.

He took a moment to reply. 'Ah, yes. Sadly, nothing left. She passed away some years ago now.'

'I'm so sorry to hear that.' I replied, feeling dreadful I'd even asked.

'Time moves on and we live and learn. You alright with that heavy load?'

I nodded as my hand gripped what felt like a belt buckle within the bag. God knows what was in there, but I was eager to find out.

While Mr Devonish was demonstrating how various fabrics and textures can be used to form a collage, I received a text from Sarah with a photo of her holding a huge bunch

THE ART GROUP

of red roses and beaming from ear to ear, and the words 'I think we're back on track. Lee seems to have come back a different person.'

I sent a smiley emoji and copious kisses and hoped she was right.

∼

Continuing to watch the demonstration, I looked at Mr Devonish's hands. They were indeed manly and practical. His chest looked muscular under his shirt too, with no man boobs, and his shoulders were broad and confidently set. I sighed and then traced his jawline with my eyes. He must have sensed me looking, because he looked up while he was ripping into some lace and we had another moment where he continued talking to the group, but fixed his eyes on me and smiled. I looked away and took my seat. It was becoming too much. I wasn't even flirting with him. It was him, not me, and I had to stop thinking I was sixteen again.

I didn't pay any attention to the demonstration. The truth is, I felt bad. All I could see were the kids' faces looking disapprovingly at me, and I was engulfed by guilt that I was even thinking of flirting with a man I knew nothing about. I had responsibilities and a family to look after. At break, I made my excuses and left early. I wanted to get home, hug the kids, and give my fantastic husband a kiss that showed him we were unbreakable. The decision made me feel better. I had to stop any crazy notion that I was a single woman or that I was even looking to be swept off my feet. Above all, I didn't like my emotions being all over the place and anyway; I had my meeting with Mum coming up and I had to get my head straight.

I walked into the house to complete silence. Ella had her head in homework at the kitchen table, and I could see Josh kicking a ball around in the back garden.

'Where's Dad?' I asked Ella, who didn't even realise I was home early.

She shrugged and said, 'Dunno. Upstairs I think?'

I checked the living room before placing my bag in the hall, then ventured upstairs. I thought he might be having a bath, but the door was wide open and there was no sign of him. The bedroom door was closed, so I opened it and saw Paul sat at my dressing table on what appeared to be a Zoom call. As I walked in, he rapidly closed his laptop and turned to face me. 'Jeez, you scared me to death,' he said, looking rosy cheeked.

'Who were you talking to?' I asked.

His response was immediate. 'No one! Anyway, why are you home so early?'

I lied. 'The teacher was ill, so we wrapped up early. Who were you talking to?'

'No one. Just a work call,' he said, picking up his laptop and standing.

'At this time of night?'

'It's not late and anyway, there's a whole team briefing tomorrow and a couple of us wanted to be one step ahead.'

'I see,' I said. 'You ended it quickly though. Did I come in at the wrong moment?'

He brushed past me. 'No, we were all done.'

I grabbed his arm. 'Do I not get a kiss when I come home these days?'

He put his arm around me while keeping his laptop between us, then gave me a peck on the cheek.

'I have been hiding a bit of a secret,' he said, breaking his half-hearted embrace.

'What?'

He rolled up his trouser leg to reveal a new tattoo. 'I had this done yesterday.'

'A devil. Why a little devil?'

'I don't know. Maybe a midlife crisis. No one will ever see it.'

'Why didn't you discuss it with me? You know I'm not keen.'

'It was an impulse thing. A couple of the lads were having them and I tagged along.'

I didn't like it and I told him so. He shrugged it off as if my opinion was irrelevant. *A little devil. Why?*

12

SESSION SEVEN

I didn't sleep a wink. My plan to have an early night and be ready for my chat with Mum backfired. Paul seemed in a strange mood. I thought it might have been me who was acting strange and that he was reacting to that. I don't like not trusting him, and I don't like myself for overthinking. Anyway, I think it was both of us. He out of nowhere, started showing an interest in the art group. Who were the other people there? Had Sarah stopped going? Why did I come home early? Were there any fit guys in the class? Did we ever paint nudes? That kind of crap.

I tried to answer genuinely, feeling he was feeling a bit jealous, and then he pushed me too far with the nude comment and I flipped. He called me a hormonal cow, and I threw a large scented candle at him. He ducked, and it smashed the glass on our wedding photo, which was on the dresser.

I had to cancel my meeting with Mum. My head was all over the place and the timing was all wrong. I needed to be fully in charge of my emotions for that one. The worst thing was, she was asking me loads of questions. I should have just kept quiet.

Sarah called and said she and Lee were heading off to Tenerife for two weeks. I wished them well, and that got me thinking about a holiday. Perhaps I might go with Paul on his golfing trip and contact a few real estate agents while I was there, save Paul a bit of legwork. I ended up in tears, because what I thought was a kind gesture, plus a chance for us to have a break from the house and the kids backfired, with Paul storming off in a huff saying it was a lad's trip and to stop being an interfering woman. I called Mum and shed a few more tears and she calmly told me that expecting everyone to be perfect was a recipe for disaster. That didn't make me feel any better about what I wanted to say to her, and I spent the rest of the day hating myself.

The local florists must have had an advertising streak, because not only did Sarah receive flowers, so did I. Paul returned early from work with a stunning bouquet of white lilies my absolute favourite. It was a thoughtful gesture, and it cleared the air between us.

The week improved, and Paul seemed more attentive. I'd missed him being interested in me, and of course, the flowers helped. I suggested we have a date night. It was long overdue, and we desperately needed to rekindle what we had before the kids were born. Paul's response was a little underwhelming. He said yes, but his comment about us being like ships in the night didn't go down well. He said the best night for him was Tuesday. The night of my art group. I nearly became very angry, but managed to stay composed, as I didn't want another week of avoiding each

THE ART GROUP

other. I texted Sarah to ask whether it was me that was being unreasonable. She responded saying the beach was lovely and the temperature a mere 29 degrees. In addition, she pointed out that the only night Paul was in was because I was out. Slightly ironic and I agreed. Funny how she is brilliant at sorting everyone else's problems, but not her own.

Anyway, I set off to the art group and, of course; I knew Sarah wouldn't be attending and, for some reason, I didn't feel I wanted to chat with the others or see Mr Devonish. Half way there, I turned around and headed home. What was I thinking? Leaving my family for a frivolous evening of self-indulgence. I needed to be with them and as Paul was home; I decided to zhuzh my hair and apply my sexiest red lipstick. He won't know what's hit him, I thought as I used my excitement to hurry myself home. I burst in the door with my skirt hitched up over my knees. In my mind, I wanted him to see me and take me there and then. Push up against the fridge and while the kids were busy with their homework, ravish me like we were wild animals.

I clocked both kids watching a film in the sitting room and rolled up my skirt from the top, just like I used to do on my way into school. Checked my hair in the hall mirror and just before I was about to kick the kitchen door wide open, I spotted Paul's hairy arse protruding from the top of his grey joggers in the dining room.

I walked in provocatively and perched on the table, exposing my legs.

'Jeez, woman, you scared me to death. What the hell are you doing home?' he said, pulling up his pants. I couldn't believe my eyes.

'What the hell is going on?' I asked, assuming a more dignified stance. All I could see were numerous cardboard boxes and Paul holding a half-assembled, hideous metal rack.

'I was going to discuss it, but everything arrived today, unexpected.'

'A gym!'

'Just a few weights and a rowing machine. I thought you might like that. Get fit and tone up a bit.'

'Fuck you,' I said, storming out.

'I was going to talk to you about it, I promise,' he shouted behind me as I bumped into Josh. 'Has Dad mentioned the snooker table?'

'No. He hasn't.'

So that was that. A dining room full of dumbbells, and a rowing machine, so I could make myself attractive again. Oh, and a snooker table for when the lads come around and treat the place like the Waggon and Horses.

13

CARMEN MIRANDA

The following evening, I arranged for Mum and Dad to meet the kids from school and cook dinner. They hadn't done it for a while, since Dad wasn't well. He said he was fighting fit, and she said she was feeling much better too. So it would be a delight to cook what Dad called chip noggins, which was the kids' favourite and something I would never entertain. Thick cut potato chips deep fried in batter. Apparently, it was a post-war staple.

I decided, and I'm not sure why, to sit in my car outside Paul's work. I wasn't spying; it was just a curious itch I had to scratch. The exit to the underground car park was my focus. It was next to the front door, so I had both angles covered. He said he would be working late and had a client meeting at 7 pm out of the office. I wanted to see if that client was really Lucy Lastic. Every time I imagined her in my mind, she had her knickers round her ankles.

Anyway, I waited and waited. No show, so I texted him to bring home some items for the kids' packed lunches. This way, he'd have to respond and might give his whereabouts away and when did a bit of emotional blackmail do any harm, especially when engrossed in espionage?

No sooner had he texted back to say he'd try but couldn't promise, the shutter door raised and out came his car. He was on his own. Lucy Lastic might be hidden under a blanket on the back seat, I thought, so I would follow.

Now this was where I discovered I wasn't cut out for the life of a secret agent. Trying to follow someone in a car without being seen and getting angry and frustrated when other cars came between us was not easy. I lost him at one point when the slowest of doddery old men stepped out on a zebra crossing and it seemed an eternity waiting for him to painstakingly make his way across. Luckily, the barrier was down at the level crossing further ahead and he was there. Ten or so cars in front, and I could see the roof of the Range Rover above all the other cars.

We headed out of town and I wondered where the hell he was going. Then I found myself right behind him. Hoping he wouldn't recognise the car, I quickly donned my sunglasses and wrapped one of Josh's yellow and red rugby shirts he'd abandoned on the back seat around my head. I looked like a very down-market and suspicious Carmen Miranda and didn't know whether I was drawing more attention my way.

He then pulled into the carpark of the technical college and as I pulled up on the street under the sprawling branches of a large conker tree, I watched him leave his car alone and go into the building. The only thing with him, his brown leather overnight bag. Mum had bought him the bag last Christmas, and he'd used it a couple of times when we

THE ART GROUP

went away. There was no briefcase, no handshakes at the door, and no female accomplice. I watched him checking himself out in all the car windows as he passed, running his hand through his hair and adjusting his belt.

Now, my brain was working overtime. The college was a weird place for him to be and I was tempted to go in and see for myself what exactly was going on in there. Then Mum called to say that Ella choked on one of Dad's chip noggins and, although she was fine; she was asking when I'd be home.

An aborted mission was frustrating to say the least, but kids first and information was power, even if I didn't know any more.

~

He rolled in gone 10 pm. No smell of booze and nothing for the kids' packed lunches. I mentioned it in a snarky comment and, knowing the kids were fast asleep, asked him about the bag. He'd conveniently left it in his car.

'I was sorting out the bedroom earlier and I was wondering where that lovely leather bag was. You know, the one mum gave you for Christmas?'

He looked at me for a moment and then helped himself to a beer from the fridge.

'Oh, that one. Yes, I use it for work now and again. You know, if I have a lot of files to cart around.'

I held back and let the silence do the talking. He took a swig of beer and couldn't look me in the eye.

'Do they still have files in a modern high-tech office?' I said confidently.

He looked at me. 'Yes, we do in our office. Anyway, what is this? The Spanish Inquisition?'

I knew this was my moment. 'No. It's just Mum said, when they were driving home, they thought they saw you up at the tech college and she remembered the bag.' Don't judge me on my economy of truth, but this was espionage at its best and I'm sure I remember Bond saying something like there are no rules in this game. And just like all the villains and henchmen, he was squirming, and I remained silent again to prolong the squirming agony even longer.

'So what was your mum doing spying on me?'

'They went from here to buy some new bedding and passed the college,' I replied.

He raised an eyebrow and swigged some more beer.

'So what were you doing at the college?'

He put his beer on the table. 'Sounds like you don't trust me?'

'Of course I trust you. It's just, you said you were at a business meeting and you're seen at a college with an overnight bag. So, just asking.'

Picking his bottle up, he turned his back and walked to the window.

'My meeting was there. We're running an intern promotion and I drew the short straw organising it.'

'Isn't that a bit below you? I thought you had assistants to do all of your donkey work?' I could tell he was backpedalling now.

'The future of our business is the up-and-coming kids. I wanted to personally inspire them.'

I nodded against my will. 'Well, you're a great inspiration to your own kids, working every hour god sends.' Shit, that was a brave move, and I waited nervously for his reply.

'It seems we are both burning the candle at both ends.'

I wasn't going to let him get away with that one. 'I go out once a week and you make it sound like I'm a neglectful mother.'

He put both hands on the table. 'Look. Things are stressful for me at work right now and I can tell you're stressed. Your dad and all that has made you tetchy. I don't think you've noticed.'

That floored me, and I couldn't help but start welling up. What I needed was a hug, and I hoped deep within my heart that he would come over and reassure me with his arms. Tell me everything was good and that he loved me.

14

SESSION EIGHT

Sarah assured me she was coming. Apparently, her holiday with Lee was a mixed bag of intense passion and arguments about his drinking and behaviour. By all accounts, she wanted to get out and let her hair down. I suggested we meet up for a proper chat. My offer of her moving in with us was always available, and I wanted her to feel safe.

Waiting in the car, I watched Mel and Trudy walking together, chatting, and then sharing a kiss. My eyes nearly popped out when surprise, surprise, Evelyn and Trevor boldly approached holding hands that they released as they entered the building. Things were definitely happening at the art group. I looked at the Twix, which was staring at me on the passenger seat, and then to the black high heels in the footwell which I'd taken in to be fixed. One heel was a little wobbly and, although they were a pair from my virtual wardrobe, they were easily in my top five. When I say virtual wardrobe, I mean the items which I love, but which rarely see the light of day. I wore the shoes at my cousin's wedding with a beautiful dress with bold sunflowers. I felt amazing that day. I'd fasted for the whole month leading up to it and it felt like I had hips once again. I have a whole wardrobe of things which I long to wear, but they stay locked away.

I could tell Sarah was troubled when she rocked up in thigh-length boots and a minidress. She looked super slim, with hips and a waist. My mind flicked to our new dining room gym and Paul's scathing comments about my weight. Maybe he was right? Maybe that's why he had stopped fancying me?

'Great boots,' I said, coveting the sleek black leather and playful tassels which clamped them tight to her legs.

'Thanks. Thought I'd give old Devonish a run for his money. I need a bit of comforting today,' she said, placing her hands on her hips and pouting.

'Don't we all,' I said, grabbing the Twix and devouring both fingers.

'You not sharing?'

'Nope!' I said, enjoying every mouthful.

Everyone stared when we walked in. Dave's eyes were out on stalks and he never acknowledge me, which was disappointing. Were men really all the same?

Devonish was already busy erecting easels and chatting and laughing with Aisha and Lila. 'Looks like you've lost him already,' I said, gesturing over to the joviality.

'I'll go over and ask him to erect my easel,' she said, pouting again.

I rolled my eyes as I watched Dave's eyes track her bottom religiously, and then Devonish turn and smile. 'You

THE ART GROUP

were both missed last week,' he said, giving a courteous nod to Sarah and then maintaining a prolonged gaze at me. I looked away and pretended to look for something in my jacket pocket. I scrunched the Twix wrapper up in my fist and felt like going to the bathroom and vomiting.

Sarah returned to her seat with a swagger and clearly trying to hide the embarrassment of Mr Devonish's rebuttal. Dave still hadn't acknowledged me, and the two of them shared a pathetic giggle.

Mr Devonish quickly took control and magically, from nowhere, produced a handful of silk blindfolds. 'This evening is all about senses. I want you to pair up and each of you take a blindfold. We look, but do we seldom see what we're looking at? Imagine being blind. How would you interpret what was in front of you? I want you to use your senses to paint a picture of your partner. Listen to them, smell them and touch them so that you understand everything about them.'

To be honest, my heart wasn't in it. I felt fat, frumpy, and finished. Everyone else in that room was living life, even Sarah, with her anxieties, was able to show vulnerability. I was washed up. Overlooked and bogged down with life. I squeezed Sarah's arm. 'I think I'm going to shoot off. Have an early night, I'm just not feeling it tonight.'

She didn't hesitate in her reply. 'No, you're not. Don't leave me all alone.'

Even if her motives were undeniably selfish, I felt like she needed me, and now I felt bad about abandoning her.

'Okay,' said Mr Devonish. 'Get into your pairs and let's get sensual.'

Trevor immediately dashed over to Evelyn, everyone

who was already paired stuck like glue and Dave made a beeline for kinky boots herself, at which she immediately snubbed me and came over all giggly and 'oh, you want to be with me?'

I looked at the door. Any feelings of guilt about leaving, gone. It was easy. All I had to do was stand up, turn my back and, without saying anything to anyone walk out of the door.

So that's what I did. Calmly took my jacket, stood and turned my back on the whole charade. 'It looks like we are paired again?' His voice was reassuring and velvety. I turned to see his beaming smile and him holding a silk blindfold.

'Yes,' I said. He took my hand and led me to my chair. 'Okay everyone. Take a blindfold and one be the model and the other the "blind" artist. Use your senses to explore their faces. Listen to them, smell and touch and use the information to form your painting. Paint instinctively, use your primeval spirit to find every feature and relay that onto your paper.' Mr Devonish came behind me and covered my eyes with the silk. I couldn't see anything and at first it was a little disconcerting. He maintained a hand on me at all times and, as he took to his seat, held my hand so that I knew I was in safe hands.

'It doesn't matter how messy you get with your paints, everyone. This is an exercise in exploration, not control.'

Fortunately, I discovered that if I looked down, I could see the floor, which helped me feel stable. I could also see Mr Devonish's feet and I noticed how clean his black leather shoes were. I liked that in a man.

The second thing I noticed was his fabulous scent. Nothing new, it had almost become his signature, but this

THE ART GROUP

time, the spicy, smoky aroma reminded me of the wood fire we sat around in Morocco. Infused cedar with incense, a hint of lavender and spice. It was earthy, and it was manly. Strong but not overpowering, and mixed with the smell of him. Call it pheromones? I don't know, but it was sublime.

'What are you sensing?' he said.

'Smell,' I replied.

'Come closer.'

He moved my hand towards his face and I noticed his knee move between my legs. My skirt being pushed up slightly. I let it happen. There was still a respectful distance between us, but his leg was tight against my inner thigh. I focussed again on the darkness of the blindfold and took my hand to his hair. It was thick and clean. As silky as the blindfold as I followed it down to his neck.

I tried to locate my paintbrush with my other hand and felt my entire arm shaking. I felt his hand take mine and place it on his cheek. I traced his stubble along his jawline, to his chin. It was defined and bold.

'Don't be afraid to explore,' he said to everyone. 'This is an art class, we are allowed to explore.'

I felt my heart in my neck and then my temples as I courageously touched his nose. It's a strange thing to feel is a nose, there's something very personal about someone else's nose.

'Don't be afraid,' he said calmly. 'I won't bite.'

I don't know why, but that line seemed to trigger something in me. I relaxed and began exploring the rest of his face with my eyes closed and started to understand what he said about seeing the 3D image of him in my mind's eye. He was a beautiful man. Proportioned perfectly and masculine. Rugged, yet refined and confident.

Not wanting to go anywhere near his eyes, in case I caused irreparable damage, I brushed my finger along his lips. Oh My God, it felt naughty. I was losing control, and I wasn't holding back. His lips were soft and slightly moist, I could feel the subtle ridges and as I explored more, his mouth opened slightly and I could feel the top of his teeth. He gently bit down. Not hard, but playfully biting, then releasing.

'You said you wouldn't bite?'

'I lied,' he said, leaning closer. Well, for some reason, that turned me upside down. In my mind, I could feel his lips meet mine. Kissing each other, without a care, intensely and passionately exploring with our tongues. I'm not sure if he was thinking the same, but I could not only hear his breathing, but I could feel it on my cheek.

The crazy thing was. And this can never get out to anyone. I was ready for him. In fact, I had never been so turned on. The combination of all my senses on red alert and that he was playing and teasing me, was something I'd been craving for a long time.

His breath came close to my cheek and that made me quiver. 'You're doing very well,' he said softly in my ear. 'Very well. Now take your brush and paint. Don't worry about colour or perspective. Just paint what you feel.'

I mean, please! Have you ever thought about what a near orgasm actually looks like? I just wanted to paint lips and tongues and, well, yes, the rest, in a rainbow of coloured bliss, which went deep into the paper. So I did.

THE ART GROUP

'Okay class. If you're ready, I want you to complete your paintings and swap blindfolds.'

OMG, I had not thought about reciprocating. I needed to leave before he just bent me over the desk and ravished me. I was ready for anything and if that knee came any closer, I might not be able to hold back.

The feeling of intense energy between us was almost unbearable as I tied the blindfold at the back of his head. We manoeuvred into the assumed position of me accommodating his knee between my legs, but this time allowed my skirt to cover his leg and not cause any unnecessary alarm to my classmates.

He leaned in close, and the smell of him instantly made my shoulders drop. His hand instinctively brushed my hair behind my ear and as he felt my lobe, he gently rubbed it, and then traced around my ear. 'Such soft skin,' he said, coming closer, and his knee perilously close to utter indecency.

He remained a gentleman and instead, ran his hand through my hair and then toyed once again with my lobe, caressing it, and then his strong hand along my jaw, just as I had done with him. His thumb etching out my cheekbone. 'High cheekbones,' he said while his head moved in tune to his hand as if playing a musical instrument.

I watched his other hand as it delicately manipulated his brush into the colour palette and then onto the paper. Gentle, yet purposeful brush strokes, on and off the paper, gliding with ease, like he was conducting an orchestra in a playful and dramatic prelude. One hand on my face and the other working its magic, illustrating and punctuating every curve and feature. Inevitably, and much to my joy, his finger on my lips gently teasing and provocatively dancing around my tongue, which I made available to him.

His brush flicked and stroked the paper as his finger toyed with my lips. I watched him biting his own lip and his eyebrows indicated the intensity of his concentration.

Oblivious to the rest of the class, I gave in to his masculinity. His masterful poise, and his attention to detail, was sublime, and I didn't care what he did to me. All I knew was I was his muse and the orchestra could play on, long after everyone had departed.

It was then, as his finger teased my tongue, I bit suggestively onto it. 'You said ...'

'I lied,' I replied.

He brought his cheek against mine. 'Naughty.'

'I can be,' I said, not caring, and then two of his fingers pushed their way between my lips and I separated them with my tongue.

'I know!' he said, knowing only I could hear.

His finished piece was remarkable. A masterpiece of playful and intense creative passion of brush strokes and paint splattered upon the page, capturing my feminine curves and my joie de vivre.

He finished by throwing off his blindfold and marvelling at my face, nodding and then the biggest, most genuine smile I have ever seen. He was a true gentleman, a naughty one, but a dignified and elegant one, who had given me something I had never experienced, and I wanted more.

I was still in a daze when I saw Sarah and Dave disappear out the door with a flippant wave and, for some reason, I purposefully delayed my own exit. I had no preconcep-

THE ART GROUP

tions of what I was waiting for, but the others all thanked Mr Devonish and made their departures.

'Would you help me to the car with some of my supplies?' he said, as if we were almost strangers. I had just had sex with him and that, to me, was quite a huge thing. Well, you know what I mean? We hadn't, but to me it felt like we had connected and his flippancy seemed almost out of character.

'Yes, sure,' I said, feeling my stomach turn. I guess I wanted him to declare his undying love for me and not discard me into the street like a ripped up and abandoned piece of blotting paper.

We reached his car and loaded it with the boxes. He turned to me and I gazed into his eyes. They were full of intention, yet darting between me and the floor.

'Look. I wanted to tell you this earlier, but with wrapping up the session etc. What I mean to say is, you have a fabulous talent. A real passion for art and I wondered if you might be interested in attending the art group trip to Paris. I think you might find it very inspirational?'

'Paris?'

'Yes, we can immerse ourselves in the beauty of Matisse and Monet with the Seine and Montmartre as our inspirational backdrop.'

'When is it and who else is going?'

He scuffed his shoe and put both hands in his pockets. 'In a couple of weeks, after the class has ended.'

I nodded. 'And ...'

He cut me off. 'I haven't asked anyone else yet.'

'I see!'

15

THE SECRET

As I said. Mum had noticed a spring in my step, and I started to look at the world slightly differently. Not sure why exactly, but that week, work seemed to flow easily. The kids were no trouble, which might have had something to do with the new snooker table? And I stopped tracking Paul's every move. I found myself looking up the Louvre and the Orangery on the internet. Just to see. I'd never been to Paris, and it all looked ... well ... romantic.

Mum said she needed a break from Dad and was coming around for a coffee. With my new found energy and outlook on life, I decided to tell her what I'd been hiding. The time was right, and I had a new vigour, which gave me courage.

'What's wrong with you? Something's changed.' No sooner had she stepped over the threshold, she was in with the questions.

'At least have a coffee in your hand before you start rabbitting on,' I said, knowing I wanted to take control.

'You've a glint in your eye. Who's given you that?'

'No one, anyway, you should know all about that.'

'What do you mean?' she said sternly.

I wasted no time. 'I've been meaning to get this off my chest for a while now and the time just hasn't been right, but I know your secret.'

Mum shook her head. 'I don't know what you're talking about.'

'I know about Dad.'

She didn't reply.

'I know all about it and, to be fair, was going to tackle this completely differently until now.'

'Go on,' she said, sipping her coffee.

'You've hidden it well all these years and I couldn't understand why you never told me the truth.'

Mum interjected. 'Just hang on a minute ...'

'No Mum. I'm saying my piece whether you like it or not.'

Her eyes shifted to the floor and I could see her gnawing on the inside of her mouth.

'I know he's not my real dad. I know that he's Jim's dad, though.'

Mum picked up her head. 'Don't go bringing your brother into this. You know I miss him being in Australia.'

'Mum, he's older than me and has a dad I thought was my dad, and who isn't. What the hell happened?'

Mum sighed. 'It was just one of those things. A holiday fling.'

'So I'm the result of a holiday fling?'

'No ... well yes, I suppose so, but it doesn't mean I think any less of you and your dad feels the same.'

'Except he's not my dad.'

THE ART GROUP

'Well, he thinks so.'

There was silence for a minute or so, and then she broke it. 'We've been through a lot over the years and you know he's not well, so don't go saying anything to him. It'll kill him.'

'What about me? When were you going to come clean about your sordid affair?'

'You don't know what it's like. I was faithful all through our marriage, except this one time. He was something else. A man you couldn't ignore. He had a power about him and he showed me attention like I never knew.'

Taking a deep breath, I closed my eyes. 'That's why you're fortunate I left it until now.'

'What do you mean?'

'Nothing. It's just ... I've been resenting both of you since I found out. I thought you were *both* hiding it from me and that Dad was just going along with it to cover your back.'

'Your dad doesn't know and he will never know.'

'It's deceitful, Mum.'

'Do you think I feel good about it?'

'I guess not, but you've been living a lie and I've been living a lie.'

It was her turn for the deep breath and together with eyes closed; she shed a tear. 'Have you met him? Your father.'

'Yes. We spoke on the phone and we met up earlier this year.'

'How ...'

'He found me on social media and said you took me away, so he couldn't see me.'

'I was married to your dad. How could I have done that? It would have destroyed everything.'

'I've been hating you Mum and I haven't liked myself as a result. You hurt me and you hurt him.'

'We've been a happy family and that would have continued if he hadn't found you.'

'You can't live a lie, mum. It's not fair to the people around you.'

The silent, frosty air between us made our coffee's go cold. Then Mum stood up and put her arms around me. 'I love you so very much. You were wanted by all of us and I tried to make things as good as I could. I've lived with the guilt and it's destroyed me at times.'

We shed a tear together and hugged like our lives depended on it.

Mum spoke again. 'So what does this change and why am I fortunate you left it longer?'

'I'm determined to try to form a relationship with Father. I owe it to him. I won't say anything to Dad. I'll spare you that. He's been incredible and I don't want him going to his deathbed with the knowledge you cheated on him.'

'That's fair enough, but you haven't answered my question.'

I paced over to the kettle. 'Do you want another coffee?'

'I want to know what's brought all this about?'

'I guess I'm just seeing life a little differently right now. A new perspective. Like I said, I've been resenting you and I didn't like what you did to both my dads. But I also know life is never straightforward. Things crop up, crazy things, and always when you least expect them.'

'So you and Paul are happy, then?'

'We have issues to work on and who knows how life will pan out, but one way or another, my plan is to be honest. No matter how it might hurt at first, I'm not prepared to live a lie.'

16

EARLY FINISH

A burst water pipe in a bank is not a good thing, especially when part of the ceiling comes crashing down onto the manager's head and narrowly misses a customer. Anyway, the result was an early finish and the prospect of a few days off, or a posting to another bank. I opted for the holiday and I had to make a decision about the art group trip.

The penultimate art group session was great fun. It was a beautiful evening, and we all ventured into the park and sketched and painted the trees, lily pond and countless people chasing dogs. We topped it off with a drink at a local bar and although I went with some expectation, Mr Devonish was a consummate professional and led the group with skill and dignity. It wasn't just him and me canoodling behind the children's climbing frame. I did, however realise, that he is a hell of a man. Confident and assured, respectful and diligent, with an amazing energy and passion for art and life. Quite inspirational and if nothing else he has influenced how I view life and relationships.

I also decided not to tell Dad, and sent Mum a huge bouquet of flowers to tell her I loved her. Another piece of good news was that Lee was attending Alcoholics Anonymous, and that Sarah was optimistic for them both. Dave had tried it on with her after the blindfold class and apparently showed her no respect, so they had a fumble and then she kicked him into touch.

It seemed the only person with a dilemma, was me. Anyway, I'm getting ahead of myself. Things came to a head when I arrived home early from the burst-pipe incident.

Not expecting anyone to be home, I was surprised to see Paul's car on the drive. Maybe they had had a burst pipe too?

The kids were at school, so I unlocked the front door quietly and assumed he might be pushing some weights or even rustling up a surprise meal for me.

No sign of him in the gym, although a mat and some weights were abandoned on the floor and no sign in the sitting room or kitchen. I tentatively ventured upstairs. The bedroom door was closed and I could hear a feint buzzing.

'Paul!' I shouted. 'If you have a woman in there, I'll never forgive you.'

Pushing the door slightly and noticing the bed was empty, I strode in boldly.

'What the hell is going on in here?'

He was completely naked in the en suite and as he turned around in shock, I couldn't help but notice the electric razor in his hand and his body almost entirely hairless.

'What are you doing home early?'

THE ART GROUP

'What are *you* doing home early and why are you shaving your body?'

He laughed. 'Oh ... yes. The lads have been talking about us doing a triathlon and it's all about aerodynamics. You know, in the pool and on the bike.'

'What on earth are you talking about? You haven't even been out for a run in the last two years, let alone cycling and swimming.'

'I've been lifting weights though.'

'Mmmmm,' I said questioning why that was relevant.

He grabbed a towel and covered himself up. 'Well, there's no better time to start. Anyway, why are you home early?'

I couldn't believe what I was seeing and the triathlon thing just wasn't cutting it with me.

'You're seeing another woman, aren't you?'

His response was immediate. 'No. No way.'

'I don't believe you. First it was the tattoo, then the late nights, now a hairless body. Something's going on.'

'There's no one else. I'm telling the truth.'

'The thing is Paul; I'm just not feeling valued anymore. You just do things without any consultation and it's making me not trust you. I need some reassurances from you or ... well I just don't know.'

Paul sighed, closed his eyes, and nodded. 'Sorry. I guess I've been under a lot of pressure at work and I haven't been thinking straight.'

'Do you love me?'

'Yes, of course. You know that.'

'I need you to tell me, Paul.'

17

DAD'S WORDS

A couple of days off work gave me time to process everything which had been racing around my head. I spent a day going around the house and standing in each room. I'm not sure exactly why, it just enabled me to think about everyone in the family and put things into perspective.

I started in Ella's bedroom. It was a bomb site as usual. I managed to find a space in the corner among her clothes, numerous cuddly animals and books. So many books. Now I understood what she meant by a TBR pile. She was an independent soul. A bookworm for sure and studious, she was going to make it in this life whatever obstacles came her way.

Apart from her disgusting bedroom, which I constantly nagged her to tidy, I wasn't concerned about her. She had a good relationship with both me and her father, which made me think about both my dads. I wanted to get to know both of them a little better as we all were ageing and I guessed time was running out for all of us.

Josh's room was in a better state, although a Lego trackway, integrated with a domino run, occupied most of the floor. He was a practical lad and his heart of gold made me smile. Lovely sweet gestures. Notes on the fridge saying 'I love you mum. PS Can we get more ice cream?' And lots of hugs and kisses gave me a warm feeling inside. I wasn't worried about him either. He might be struggling at school, but I knew his interpersonal skills would see him win through whatever he decided upon.

Giving the bathroom a wide berth, I ended up in our room. I'd made the bed and arranged all my show cushions and a throw, so it looked like something from Homes & Gardens. Not that it made the feel of the room any better. The en suite door was wide open. I could see Paul's towel on the floor and hairs still covering every surface.

This wasn't what I envisaged from a marriage. We used to be so much in love. He bent over backwards to woo me, and I loved that. Nothing was ever too much trouble, and I truly felt like he loved me. I glanced over at our wedding photograph on the dresser. The glass still cracked, I looked so much younger and slimmer. Paul's smile was infectious. I remember it was the first thing I liked about him. So much fun and never-ending jokes, he made my sides split with laughter. Standing behind us, both his parents, long gone now, and mine. Not my real dad, obviously.

My resentment of them had almost petered out to nothing. I'm glad Mum and I had our heart to heart. I could understand how she felt and how it could happen. After all, I was on the verge of something potentially life changing

THE ART GROUP

myself and the words of my real father came straight to mind.

I met with him a couple of times. He's in Scotland, so not easy to just pop in for coffee. He was a proud man, a gentleman and very happy to see me. He'd been in the dark, as Mum sheltered me from the truth. When we met, he expressed his disappointment in how Mum had managed the situation, yet he appeared philosophical too. We hugged, and he said that we should have no regrets in life, that we should be true to ourselves and to not compromise ourselves, no matter how hard that might seem.

I respected him for that and held onto his words. Life was not for standing still and squandering being unhappy and bitter. That was a waste.

I spent time in the kitchen, the dining room and the greenhouse and then poured myself a G&T and went up to the bedroom.

It felt decadent and naughty having a drink at eleven-thirty in the morning, but what the hell.

Reaching for my little under-seat bag, I remembered the times I'd had a drink in the airport in the morning and what was wrong with that?

Unzipping it released that holiday smell. A mix of sun cream, warm sunshine and freshly ironed clothes. I sat next to it on the bed and let my mind wander. The Champs-Élysées, Moulin Rouge and sophisticated cocktails by the Seine. I missed the romance, craved the passion, and was excited by the possibilities of love, being loved and ultimately cherished so much that my heart sang every day. I wanted that, and I deserved it.

Picking my red stilettos from my collection, I tossed

them frivolously into the bag and then followed them with lace matching underwear and the silk nighty I was saving for a special occasion. That felt naughty and liberating in itself and I had no trouble filling the remainder of the bag with my most favourite clothes and some I'd never worn, from my 'virtual' wardrobe, which was even more exciting.

That leads me to my dilemma. Which shoes should I wear for the flight? Not the stilettos, they are bedroom shoes. No, something practical, but sexy. Shoes I can walk up gangplanks with yet show a little sophistication. Choices, choices. Sandals no, trainers, definitely not. Work shoes were too boring and Converse too grungy. Another pair of ridiculously sexy high heels for sure would go in just in case, but for travelling, I decided on boots. I have a pair with a heel and they are tight to my calves. Playful, yet sophisticated and as practical as is possible given the style. No more agonising, the decision was made and I would wear them that evening for the last art group session and a trial run. Hopefully, Sarah would have toned down her look and not overshadow me.

A text to her saying I was playing things down, was my devious plan, but I had nothing to fear as she said she'd heard it was a life drawing session and because Lee had a few issues with her attending, she was giving it a miss, but to say bye to everyone there for her. I agreed and then swiftly zipped the case and placed it back in the bottom of the wardrobe under the Christmas decs.

18

SESSION NINE

You're almost up to date. Apologies for taking the long route to explain, but there I was, in calf-hugging boots and about to walk into class. I was nervous. Didn't want to make a fool of myself and a quick reassurance from Mr Devonish would be greatly appreciated, if not essential. The note in my pocket, if the response was good, read. *Thank you for a superbly inspiring and life-changing class. You are an amazing man and I'm very much looking forward to the group trip. Catherine X.*

Of course, I had a plan-B. Keep the note securely in my pocket and unpack the case as soon as I returned home. Paul was out anyway. A not very surprising business meeting, so he wouldn't be back until late and Mum was on babysitting duty. That would give me a chance to sort it when I got back and no one would be any the wiser. Anyway, I was focussing on Plan-A and entered the class with trepidation but also optimism.

No Sarah, no Dave, Evelyn and Trevor sitting together

and Mr Devonish standing proudly at the front in a black roll-neck jumper and black jeans. I could have scoffed a whole box of Milk Tray without even taking my eyes off him. He was gorgeous. Simple as that, and my heart was thumping.

He clocked me as soon as I walked in, and as I took my seat, he calmly and confidently approached and gave me the most incredible smile. 'It's good to see you,' he said, looking into my eyes.

I instantly took the note from my pocket and handed it to him. Shielding the rest of the group with his back, he took my hand and removed the note while maintaining a hold. I could feel his magnetism and energy surging from his body into mine, and I was smitten. All the same feelings I had experienced when we were exploring each other the previous week and a smile and an air of 'I want you' were well received, and I wanted him.

He read the note and nodded. His eyes never faltered from mine and I knew it was game on.

It was only when he returned to the front, did I question what in Milk Tray heaven I was about to do. No one else had mentioned the trip, and I knew full well they were not invited.

Was I making a stupid mistake? Was this potentially the end of my marriage? What about the kids? Was this me, just rebelling against my dad thing? Or was I feeling neglected and lied to by Paul?

The words of my father came to me. 'Be true to yourself.' I had to do that, for his sake, and for my own sake. I was worth it and was no longer prepared to play second fiddle to anyone.

THE ART GROUP

'Okay everyone. It's our last session, and I thought it would be a treat, if not a slightly cheeky one, to have a life model in this evening and to bring all our new found knowledge together for this final piece. No touching though, this time!' He said, looking directly at me.

God, he was exciting.

'I want you to gather all your equipment. Paints, pencils, charcoal, acrylic, leather and lace and feel free to use whatever medium and style takes your fancy. But, please remember, the model is a professional. Someone who is used to being naked in front of class and we should show them the respect they deserve. So no obscenities, or laughing, please. I'll lower the lights and bring him in behind the screen and then, when everyone is comfortable, we can either ask him to sit or stand. I'll leave that to you to decide once the screen is removed.'

A man! Jeez, I wasn't expecting a man. To be honest, I'd personally rather see Mr Devonish strip off and I could just ogle and daub paint with abandon wherever my interest was greatest.

With a dimming of the lights, Mr Devonish escorted the model through a side door and behind a skillfully erected screen which just showed his lower legs.

I've always seen feet as a strange part of the body and his were no exception. Rather long and bony. Not an attractive feature at all.

No hairs either, which for me was a shame. I do like a hairy man, particularly a hairy chest and forearms. I can take or leave a hairy back, but hairy legs look stronger and fitter somehow.

I assembled my acrylics. I was in the mood for some

colour and texture, and I purposefully positioned another chair next to me so that if Mr Devonish was to come and offer some of his creative flair, I could accommodate him without any fuss.

I prepared my pallet and chose a large, stout brush. I wasn't sure why.

The model shuffled around. He was obviously removing the rest of his clothes and there was a bit of tittering from Patty, who was then, in turn, causing others to giggle.

Mr Devonish soon quashed any frivolity, and it was then, I saw something which nearly paralysed me. A tattoo on the man's leg, which I had not previously noticed. A tattoo of a little devil holding a trident.

I felt my blood plummeting to my feet. The devil looked familiar, which made my heart temporarily stop beating and everything appeared in slow motion as the model walked out from behind to reveal himself.

Mr Devonish showed him to a box with a black sheet over and asked if we would prefer sitting or standing? I didn't hear the decision. The world had almost stopped spinning and as my eyes focussed on his face; I felt myself retching. It was Paul. My completely hairless and butt naked husband Paul right in front of all my classmates and Mr Devonish. I hid behind my easel and continued to retch.

Was this some kind of cruel joke? Why was he doing this to me?

I was trapped behind my easel. What could I do? Stand up and shout at him? That would embarrass everyone.

Make myself obvious and stare him out? Or gracefully pack up my things and leave? Either way, we had some serious talking to do, and I was far from happy.

19

KILLER HEELS

So, here I am in my killer heels. I decided not to go with the boots and went straight for the highest, sexiest shoes I owned and, of course, they were my Louboutins. Black with the red sole. A little pastiche or demode, some Parisienne's may say, but I felt great in them and I had the whole ensemble to match from holdups to pushups and I was feeling amazing. I deserved to feel amazing. I'd been in a hole for too long. A hole where I was just bumbling, along with no great purpose other than being a mundane wife and mother.

Today is different, today is liberating, and I'm celebrating my own beauty. It's safe to say that the events over the last few weeks have been both liberating and empowering. Mr Devonish, or Degas as I know him now, stepped into my life just when I needed him. By the way, his mother must have known he would become an artist, and they do say, you become your name, but Degas Devonish does suit him.

Anyway, I have him to thank for everything. Without him I would still be plain and frumpy Cathy, who was pushed around and treated like a dried-out dishcloth. To feel beautiful and enchanting is every girl's dream, and the dream became reality. Not only that, I have started feeling feminine again and prepared to show my vulnerabilities, instead of always trying to be strong and in control of every single detail in life.

I can do all that, but it's so refreshing to allow yourself to be vulnerable and let your man take the lead with respect and dignity.

Obviously, I found out that Paul wasn't seeing another woman. He was sneaking out to be a life model in art classes. Why the hell he didn't tell me before is baffling. It would have saved a lot of heartache and embarrassment.

A midlife crisis he called it. Himself not feeling confident about his own body.

I always thought he was overconfident to the point of arrogance, but it turns out the pressure from the lad's group and work associates made him feel inferior. He declared that there was no promotion. He was passed over for Lucy, who had become his boss. He was too embarrassed to tell anyone and instead kept the pretence. Sad that the villa in the Algarve was never really on the cards, but in a strange way, I understand what he was going through. Confusion and anger, just like I felt against Mum and Dad.

You do stupid things when you're confused and modern life puts unrealistic expectations upon us sometimes and I guess he had to give the impression he was still a man or he would lose all respect.

I say he should have spoken out about it before, but I

THE ART GROUP

wonder what the conversations would have been like. Maybe in a bizarre way, things come to a crescendo for a reason. Because you are forced to respond, and in emergency mode.

I have to say, my feet are killing me. I've a blister on my left heel and my toes think they've been amputated, but the sun on the water as the boats go by is such a delight and the hustle and bustle of the city is exciting. We're on our way to the Louvre and I have hinted severely that a coffee and a pain au chocolat will be happening as soon as possible, before I throw the Louboutins in the Seine and he has to carry me.

What I've learned is that my father was right. You have to be true to yourself. Life is too short to waste time with regrets or apathy. You have to make things happen and forever seeking happiness, well that's an unrealistic goal, really. It's better to live the best life you can, follow your dreams as best you can and be proud of who you are and the decisions you make. Then, and only then, will you happen upon moments of happiness, and it's those times you have to be grateful for.

Hold on a minute, he's just squeezed my hand, kissed me and is escorting me to a fabulous little veranda overlooking the river with the cutest of tables with red gingham tablecloths and fresh flowers.

I'm feeling lucky and I'm grateful, strangely, for all the turmoil of the last few months. I think I appreciate the kids more, especially when they are at home, but I know I need a man in my life who has faults and is learning, like me. Has confidence, yes, but also shows a little vulnerability. I guess communication is the key. He's gone in for the coffee and

I've changed my mind at the last minute for a tarte au pomme.

It's a journey for both of us and that takes courage. Courage to challenge your beliefs and insecurities, to push the boundaries of who we are. I feel stronger and wiser now.

Hang on, he's coming with the tray. He does look handsome. Maybe it's the way he's looking at me? I don't know?

'Coffee and tarte au pomme.'

'Thanks Paul, I love you.'

20

I KNOW WHAT YOU'RE THINKING

Did I make the right decision? Well, hindsight is a wonderful thing, that's for sure, and some might say, we learn the hard way.

Despite having virtually no skin left on the back of my heels, and my left bunion feeling like I have termites burrowing into my foot. The heels were perfect. I caught sight of my calf in a shop-window reflection, and it made me smile. I felt confident in them, but also, I felt empowered.

I realised I was absorbed in my own self-pity regarding Dad and was blaming everyone else. Mum and I cleared the air, and we both said we should have spoken about it a long time ago. There's a sense of relief, and strangely we have become closer. Dad, sadly, passed away a couple of weeks ago. We were all with him, and I remained his daughter right up to his last breath. There was no reason to rock the boat and make him suffer any more than he was already. I held his hand as he left us. He was a good man, and I always felt his unconditional love.

I've been in touch with my real dad since, and we are planning to meet up at some point. Which feels like the right thing to do, and Mum seems fine with it.

I've just about caught up, except to tell you that, obviously, Paul and I had a fabulous time in Paris. Things seemed to change between us. Yet again, we said we should have talked sooner. I hadn't appreciated what he was going through at work and how that affected his self-confidence. I think it was a cry for help in many ways. A midlife crisis?

To be completely honest, I still can't understand why he did the life-modelling thing. It seems bizarre to me that anyone suffering from confidence issues would want to strip bare in front of strangers. You wouldn't catch me doing anything like it. Mum said she thinks he needs help.

Anyway, as I said, things have changed, and we are at least communicating. I wouldn't say things are amazing. Far from it, but we are giving it a go.

I'm writing this from my new desk in the dining room. I rallied Paul and the kids to clean out the garage and, with the help from some LED lighting and a couple of speakers, it's now the gym/snooker/games/party room and I have a wonderful creative space, which looks out onto the garden. My easel takes pride of place and I have all my art supplies to hand, ready for when inspiration strikes. I decided it was time for the kids to show more respect for me and the house. They grumbled, of course at having to tidy up and undertake some manual labour, but I noticed how the three of them, seemed to enjoy working together with a common purpose. I'm no longer going to roll over just to make the

THE ART GROUP

peace. I shall not make my main aim their comfort and luxury.

Instead, I have a sanctuary. A place I can use when I need to offload stress and be creative. But it's more than that. Not just a place, but a chance to reflect and respect my own needs. After all, respect comes from self-respect, and this is the start of a new era for me.

I'll write to you again and keep you posted on how things turn out, and I'm pretty sure that Sarah will be in touch soon, with what is happening in her life. I have to be strong for her too at the moment, but, anyway, I'll leave it to her to fill you in.

So, that's it, except to say that I felt I needed to carry on exploring my creativity and Mr Devonish has kindly offered to squeeze me in for some one to one tuition. Our first session is next week. Wish me luck.

The End.

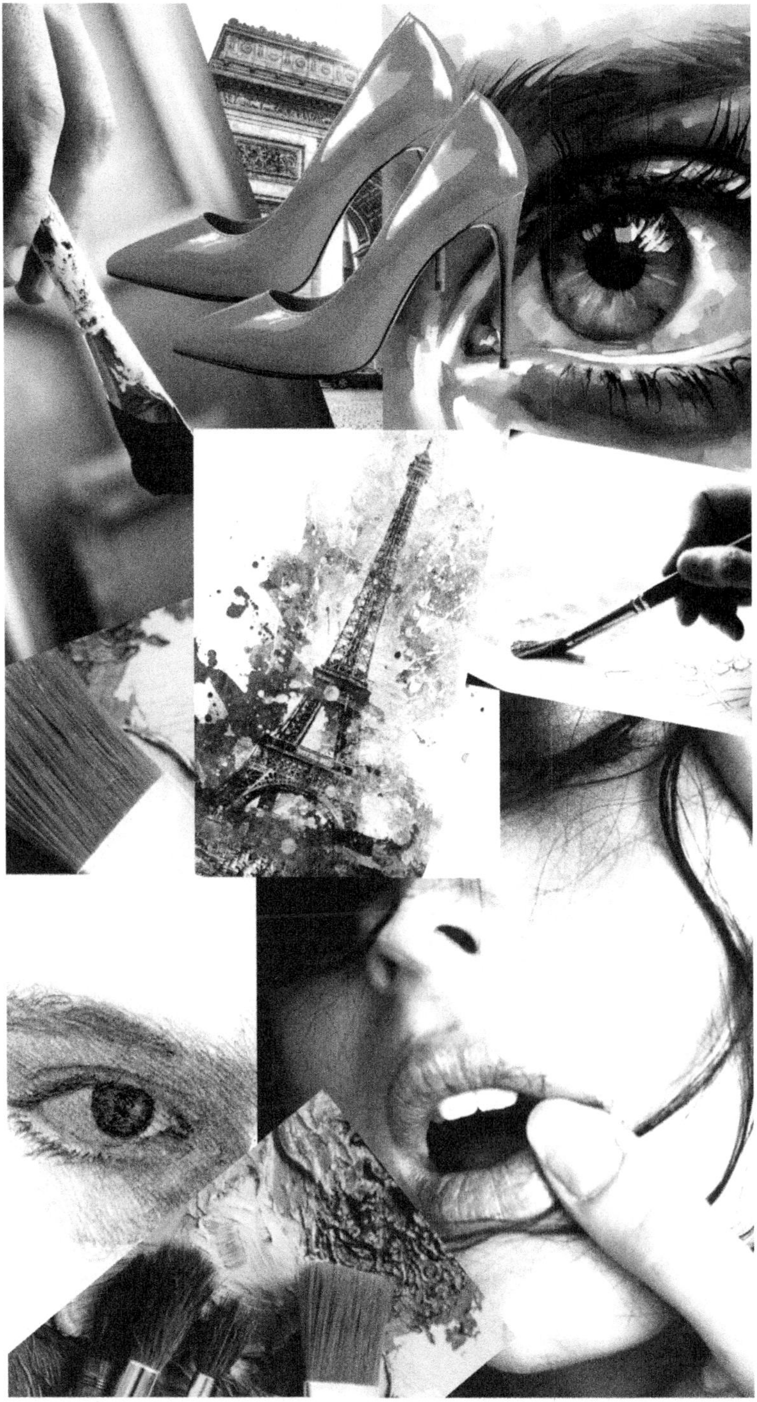

ABOUT THE AUTHOR

I was born in Yorkshire, England, in 1969. I kept my creative passion locked up for many years. Now, I am free to express my creativity in my writing, in the hope I might set others free from their personal prisons, whatever they are? It's okay to be you. Be proud.

If you enjoyed reading this book, please consider leaving an honest review on your favourite platform. I would be eternally grateful. Good reviews will help the algorithms to recognise my work and help other readers to discover new books.

More information about my dyslexia, and how I had never read a book before becoming an author, can be found at
www.jacrawshaw.com

- youtube.com/@jacrawshaw
- instagram.com/j_a_crawshaw_author
- goodreads.com/J_A_Crawshaw
- tiktok.com/@j_a_crawshaw_author
- facebook.com/jacrawshawbooks

ALSO BY J A CRAWSHAW

The Swing. 1st in series. The Life Changing Fiction Series.

The View Beyond. 2nd in series and sequel to The Swing.

The Void Between Words. My laid bare, gritty and humorous story of possibly the worlds most unlikely author. My dyslexic journey from non reader to author.

Poetry From The Heart. Abstract mind mumblings in poetry form.

For more information about all my books, events and insider knowledge on forthcoming events, visit my website

www.jacrawshaw.com

REVIEWS

We all value reviews, but seldom leave them.
Less than 1% of readers leave a review, so when I receive one, I'm thrilled. I mean, really thrilled, to the point, I leap around the room and become emotional.
I would be incredibly grateful and honoured to receive feedback on any store, platform or social media site.
Here are reasons why it's so important to me.

1. I can improve my writing, so you enjoy it more.
2. I know if I'm on the right track in terms of what you like to read.
3. It gives me confidence to carry on writing.
4. It makes the book more visible to other readers by convincing the algorithm its worthy.
5. It makes us writers feel loved and I'd like to share that love with you.

Thank you

Click Link To Review

Printed in Great Britain
by Amazon